MONEY BREEDS ENVY

TORICA TYMES

DAVID WEAVER PRESENTS 2022

ONE
MONEY BREEDS ENVY

Ivory sat behind the wheel of the car in total shock and disbelief. The sound of the sirens swirled around at the pit of his soul. The red and blue flashing lights flipped on a panic switch, and his heart began to race at a rapid pace. At that very moment, Ivory knew the part of the game that no one wanted to play, was now here and present.

His spirit shook with nervousness, as the thought of many years behind bars began to creep inside of his mind. Just as he glanced over at his ride or die chic, Tweety, once again the voice of an officer could clearly be heard shouting out commands thru a P.A. system.

"Turn off the ignition and toss the keys out of the window! Then keep your hands where I can see them and slowly exit the vehicle!"

Ivory quickly looked from his right and left, then stared up into the rear-view mirror. The car was surrounded by what seemed to be dozens of police officers. He knew there was nothing slick he could pull to get out of this one. He only hoped that Jesup, his lawyer was able to work a miracle. However, with a trunk full of cocaine, he knew his chances were slim to none.

For a split second, Ivory dropped his head into the palms of his hands, then halfway complied with the officer's commands. He slung the keys out of the window, after turning off the car, but he wasn't ready to feel those steel cuffs shackling his wrist. The next second, he swiftly turned his focus back over towards Tweety, and continued looking at her, as if it was the last time he would ever see her in life again.

She was sitting in silence, as her body trembled with fear. With her head held low, the tears fluently streamed down her face. Seeing his Queen cry crushed Ivory's heart, and pride to the fullest. He had failed to protect her from harm's way, even though Tweety had insisted on playing her role, as that ride or die type of chic.

However, now, there was nothing he could say that would wipe away the tears from flooding Tweety's face. Regardless, Ivory had to let her know one last time just how much he felt for her. In a saddened tone of voice, filled with pain, Ivory softly spoke.

"Tweety, I love you with all my heart. Now, I don't know what tomorrow will bring for me, but my feelings for you will never change."

If Tweety's tears had been fire, then Ivory's words were gas being poured onto the flames. She covered her face with the palms of her hands, then burst out crying like a newborn crack baby. Tweety couldn't even bring herself to look in Ivory's direction. She sharply turned her head to the right, and sadly stared out of the passenger window. The sound of Tweety's cries continued to rise in volume, and the tears were falling so fast, and heavy that they had begun to dampen the blouse she was wearing. Just as, Ivory was about to reach over to console Tweety, once again, the voice of the police officer could be heard.

"Driver! Place both hands out of the window and exit the vehicle!"

Ivory shook his head from side to side, then extended his right hand, and placed it onto Tweety's left shoulder. However, to his surprise, his touch seemed to startle her. She shrugged away his attempt to show affection, which dearly hurt his heart.

"Tweety...Tweety, talk to me."

Ivory quickly pleaded with her to speak but at the moment, she didn't know what to say or how to feel.

"Driver! Both hands out of the car, now!"

Surprisingly, the voice of the officer is what finally compelled Tweety to turn towards Ivory to speak. With the tracks of her tears still racing down her face, she took a long, deep breath, exhaled it slowly, then spoke in between her sniffling cries.

"Bae, I don't want this to get any worse than it already is so just do what the man said."

Her words brought Ivory to the complete realization of the situation. Without any hesitation, Ivory slowly nodded his head up and down. Before fully complying with the officers, he leaned over and placed a gentle kiss upon Tweety's forehead, then quickly said his final words to her.

"Tweety, don't you worry about me. You just do whatever you have to do, to make it home safe, and make your dreams happen."

The next moment, he exited the car with both hands held high in the air. With their guns locked, loaded, and aimed directly at his head, the officers carefully approached, handcuffed, and arrested Ivory. As they walked him to their car, Ivory took one last look back over his shoulder to get another glimpse of Tweety. What he saw only caused his soul more pain. His heart dropped to the pit of his stomach, as he witnessed Tweety being escorted to a squad car in handcuffs. Only hours earlier, he had planned for this to perhaps be his final trip, but he never imagined it would end like this.

His first cousin, Frost was dead. Tweety was in handcuffs. Now, weighing heavy on his head was the lengthy prison sentence that he faced. The game was over.

A couple of hours later, Tweety was sniffling, and shivering inside of a small interrogation room. From the first moment the detectives strutted through the door, they were threatening to charge her with the trunk full of coke as well, unless she cooperated.

"Save your own ass, Ms. Barkley. Ivory Phillips is done on the streets. The only thing he'll be running is his ass to the chow hall for the next ten to twenty years. No need for you to go down with him."

To allow his words to fully soak in, the detective momentarily paused, before continuing to speak. With sheer seriousness written all over his face, he spoke in a firm tone of voice.

"So, what is it going to be, Ms. Barkley? Are you ready to write your statement?"

Tweety smacked her lips, and rolled her eyes at the detective, then began to speak in a sassy manner.

"Yes, today my name is Ms. Barkley, but one day it'll be Mrs. Phillips. Therefore, I ain't writing a damn thang down. Did I say enough for y'all yet?"

Simultaneously, both of the detectives faces turned redder than Rudolph's nose. In a loud rage, detective number two attempted to break Tweety.

"Lady! This isn't a damm joke! It's seriously your last chance to walk out of here as a free woman!"

Tweety understood they already knew Ivory was the mastermind of the operation. They knew his whole damn crew but to Tweety, it just didn't feel right speaking to the police about illegal moves her man had made. However, Ivory's last words to her kept repeating over and over inside of Tweety's mind. It was as if she could hear Ivory sitting right next to her. Suddenly, the door to the interrogation room flew open, and two well-dressed men in black suits entered. Before turning their attention towards Tweety, the first man quickly introduced himself and his partner, then in a blunt manner gave the two detectives instructions.

"Hello, gentlemen. I'm Federal Agent Baxley, and this is my partner, Agent Conner. We'll be taking over for the time being. Now, please give us the room."

With a smug look on their faces, the two detectives exited the interrogation room without saying anything. The second Tweety heard the words "federal agent", she instantly tensed up. She had never moved a single gram of dope, but simply from being Hernandez's daughter, and

Ivory's lady, she had learned long ago, that when the Feds get involved, there's no time for games to be played. While Agent Conner stood in the corner of the room in silence with his arms folded, Agent Baxley proceeded to take a seat directly across from Tweety. Unlike the first two detectives, the federal agents weren't concerned with getting a statement written against Ivory. They had desires to hook a bigger fish.

"Good evening, Tweety. You don't mind me calling you Tweety, do you?"

The second Agent Baxley uttered the name Tweety, she felt a state of shock run through her soul. By him calling out her nickname, it further gave her confirmation that the Feds knew every detail associated with Ivory. They had certainly done their homework, or someone had been talking. With a billion butterflies floating within, Tweety attempted to remain calm, cool, and collected. She quickly painted an unbothered expression on her face, as she answered Agent Baxley's question in a smart mouth manner.

"Do I mind you calling me Tweety? Umm that's my damn name, ain't it?"

Agent Baxley slowly shook his head from side to side, then proceeded to look over his shoulder at his partner. Without verbally communicating, at that moment Agent Conner knew to take the lead.

"Ok, Tweety, enough of the tough girl act. With all the coke Ivory was busted with, we don't need any help from you. Technically, we could put the same charges on you that your boyfriend has against him. However, we're not here for you nor Ivory."

With a face filled with frowns, Tweety immediately replied the second Agent Conner spoke his last word.

"Well, what in the hell do y'all want?"

"Your Uncle Felix, also known as Mr. Mexico. We've been trying to put him away for nearly a decade now, but nothing will stick, and sadly enough, anyone that cooperated with us soon disappeared, or was murdered."

With a straight face, Tweety looked Agent Conner square in the eyes for a solid five seconds without saying a word. The next moment, she suddenly burst out crying with laughter. She continued to chuckle, as she started her reply.

"Give you my Uncle? Man please, y'all might as well lock my black ass up now. Niece or not, snitches get dumped in ditches, and I'm not ready to die for being a rat."

Anger Conner quickly nodded his head up and down, then just as fast, he rose from his seat. The moment the agents were about to walk out of the interrogation room, their commander entered, and briefly spoke before exiting.

"She's not going to talk. Cut her loose and let her go home. I just sent a couple of officers out to secure our informant, so feel free to use that when you two speak with Mr. Phillips. He might start talking, and give us his connect, once he finds out we got him dead to right."

On his way out, Agent Baxley spoke in a spiteful manner towards Tweety.

"I hope you never see Ivory another day in your life. There's no guarantee someone will come home while doing years of hard prison time."

Tweety was free to go but her body was momentarily frozen to the seat. The agent's words hit her soul like a ton of bricks, and now the reality of the situation was fully setting in. She wanted, and needed to hear Ivory's voice, but knew that wouldn't happen tonight.

As Tweety was walking out of the precinct, she pulled her phone from her purse, but she truly had no idea who she was going to call, besides a ride. Her thoughts were racing a mile a minute, pondering how this all occurred. In her heart, she just knew her best friend wouldn't betray her in such a manner. Although, in the back of her mind, she couldn't help but wonder did Mea really snitch, and tip the law off about Ivory's last run. After hopping in the backseat of a cab, Tweety decided to send a text to Mea's cell.

"Hey girl, I'm sure you heard about what went down with me and

Ivory but I'm headed home now. Are you at my place? If not, where are you?"

Every second that elapsed after pressing send, Tweety sat there impatiently starring at the screen of her phone. Only five full minutes had passed by, but to Tweety, it felt more like fifty-five. Growing more and more anxious by the second, she finally decided to give Mea a call. However, there wasn't a single ring, as the phone went straight to voicemail. Her heart skipped a beat from not hearing Mea pick up. Tweety didn't know what to do, but she knew that she had to quickly gather her composure. Minutes later, she arrived home to an empty house. Part of her was hoping Mea would be on her couch, in a deep sleep, but that wasn't the case.

She was afraid to call her uncle, she couldn't call Ivory, and there were no signs of Mea anywhere. At that moment, Tweety decided to try and give Ray a call. On the first ring, Ray answered the phone in an anxious tone of voice. He assumed he was speaking to Ivory. Ray was so extremely ready to work, that he reeled off three quick questions before Tweety could get a word in.

"What's good, Ivory!? You back in the city? Where I need to be to pick up that work?"

There was a moment of dead silence, before Tweety replied. She cleared her throat, then proceeded to tell Ray all about her last few hours.

"Ray, this Tweety. Ivory got locked up. Them folks were deep and waiting for us to pull up in my yard."

"What the fuck!? Shit!" Ray yelled out in anger.

"Exactly! I don't know what to do now." Tweety replied in a lost tone of voice.

"Everything is going to work out in our favor, just watch." Ray attempted to calm and console Tweety.

"I hope you're right. But Ray, have you been thru the projects in the last hour or so? I'm trying to find Mea. She was supposed to be here at my place when we got back but there's no sign of her anywhere."

Ray briefly hesitated before responding to Tweety's question about where Mea may be.

"Umm, Tweety, I seriously doubt anyone we know has seen Mea in the last hour...and just being honest, I'm pretty sure no one ever will again. Ya dig?"

Tweety totally understood what Ray was hinting at but couldn't gather herself fast enough to reply before Ray continued to talk. She just didn't want to believe her friend was gone.

"Tweety, just stay put, and I'm going to head your way now. If you already haven't, go ahead, and give Jesup a call. Get him caught up on everything that went down."

After the phone call ended, she momentarily stood frozen, reminiscing on the good times her and Mea had during their friendship. Deep down in her soul, she wanted to believe that Mea wasn't the reason Ivory was sitting in a cage but knew oh too well that Ray wouldn't have done such a deed without feeling it was necessary. Tweety snapped out of her daze, then quickly went to shedding tears, after looking up to see the oil painting of her and Ivory on the wall. She slowly made her way over towards the sofa and flopped down in a lifeless manner.

In the back of her mind, all she could hear was one of the conversations that they had earlier replaying over and over in her head. Ivory was going to give the game up and open her salon. Remembering the happy look that he had while explaining his visions to her made a trace of a smile shine through the tracks of tears. Tweety was still overwhelmed by what had happened to Ivory, as well as her friend Mea, but she knew she had to hold it all together, and quickly get in touch with Attorney Jesup.

———

MEANWHILE, back in Bowling Park, Jit, and Dunn Dunn were handling business as usual. The trap was jumping like Jordan in his prime, as their customers formed lines longer than the ones people waited in at Six Flags. Money was coming in at a rapid pace, as if they were running a Las Vegas casino. The package Jolly Jr. had not too long ago dropped off was quickly being distributed to the streets.

Keysha was out, and about making deliveries to smaller trap houses throughout the city, when suddenly her phone started to ring. While flashing an expression of frustration on her face, Keysha's eyes squinted with confusion, as she looked at the caller ID. After allowing the phone to ring for a while, Keysha finally answered the call in a very harsh manner, and a tone of voice that matched.

"Who the fuck is this!?"

"What up Keysha! This your boy Byron. I need an ounce of that real good dope y'all been serving lately."

Byron was born and raised in Bowling Park, but never taken too seriously, by any of the real hustlers in the city. He was a part time drug dealer, and a full-time liar about how much dope he really sold. If the truth be told, he only sold enough crack to pay for his coke habit. Keysha had been serving him, ever since Jit fell out with Byron over an ounce that he had fronted to him for a week. A week that never came.

"Yeah, but why the hell you calling from this weird ass number?"

For a solid few seconds, there was a brief pause of complete silence before Byron replied.

"Cause of a stalking ass bitch. I just changed my number, so go ahead and lock this one in your phone."

"Ok, whatever Playboy. In about fifteen minutes meet me at The Circle K on the corner of Forrest and Floyd Road."

"Bet. 'Ppreciate that Keysha."

As soon as the call ended, Byron quickly turned around to face the person standing behind him. The moment the two locked eyes, Byron began to loudly speak in an excited, and confident tone of voice.

"A piece of cake! I told you, bruh! Now let's go see if you can make this lick happen!"

Ten minutes later, Byron and his partner Bear was pulling into the convenience store that Keysha had suggested. To get a better view of the traffic coming into the lot, Byron backed his car into a parking spot on the side of the store. At the same time, his partner in crime lit a blunt that was in the ashtray.

Bear had only been out of prison for a month. He had served a ten-year bid for armed robbery, and didn't give the first fuck about going back. The complexion of his skin was blacker than the darkest night, and Bear stood six feet, six inches tall, and weighed over 300 pounds. His only concern was getting his hands on a bag of cash to spend, and a stash of dope to get high with. The two had only been at the convenience store a solid two minutes before an overanxious Bear began to get impatient. He took a long, hard pull from the blunt, then slowly exhaled the smoke, before he began to speak.

"Say, Byron, where the fuck this bitch at bruh!"

"Pump your brakes Big Boy. She'll be pulling up any minute now."

Just as soon as Byron finished replying, Keysha was turning into the convenience store. With her high-tech car stereo system booming trap music, Keysha parked at gas pump number 2. Her radio was blasting so loud, to the point that the sound sent vibrations thru the car Byron and Bear was sitting in.

"Told you, bruh. There Keysha go right there."

As Byron hopped from his ride, and began walking towards Keysha, Bear also hurried his large body out of the car, and quickly made his way into position. Just as Keysha was about to give Byron a call, she was somewhat startled, as he started to tap on her passenger window.

As Keysha let the window down, she loudly yelled out.

"Damn, Byron! Boy you snuck up on a bitch then. I didn't even see your ass coming my way."

Byron flashed a fake smile, and began to apologize, as he opened the passenger door to Keysha's car.

"My bad, Keysha. I didn't mean to scare you."

"Hold up now, uma Bonecrusher type of bitch. I ain't never scared nigga." Keysha replied with a slight smirk on her face, as she whipped out her digital scale.

While she was weighing up the cocaine, Byron's eyes began to get bigger than baseballs. The junky inside of him couldn't hardly wait to do a line of that clean, good coke. Suddenly, the entire car shook, as Bear forcefully snatched the rear driver's side door open, and quickly maneuvered his extra-large body into the backseat.

Even before Keysha could react in any form or fashion, Bear had a fistful of her dreads with one hand and placed the barrel of a small handgun at the back of her head with the other. In a split second, Bear aggressively tightened up his grip on Keysha's dreads. The next moment, he looked at the back of Byron's head and began to shout out instructions.

"Ay, fuck nigga, slowly turn your ass around, and look at me!"

The intensity of Bear's voice sounded so believable that Byron had seriously started to worry about what would happen next. As frowns of fright formed on his face, Byron cautiously began to rotate his neck towards Bear. Once the two were staring at one another, Bear quickly winked his eye, as he continued to bark out instructions, in a loud tone of voice.

"Empty your muthafuckin pockets and get your pussy ass out the car."

With the barrel of a small handgun pressed flush against the back of Keysha's head, she didn't make any sudden moves. However, she quickly cut her eyes over at Byron, and spoke her mind, as he had started to drop his money on the front seat of the car.

"Bruh, I know a set up when I see it. If he let me live, then you gon die."

The very moment Keysha ended her words, Bear swiftly used the handgun to strike her over the head. As blood began to gush, Keysha's body slowly slumped over onto the front seat. Byron quickly hopped out of the car, as if nothing had just happened, then made his way back to his ride. Bear maneuvered his big body out of the backseat as fast as possible. He opened the driver's door, and mushed Keysha's motionless body over, then started up the car's engine. Before he placed the car into gear, Bear gathered all the dope, and money into a small bag, then peeled out of the parking lot.

Byron quickly followed Keysha's car away from the store. Bear only drove about two blocks down, before turning into Able Homes Housing Projects, and parked near the trash dumpsters. Before getting out, Bear looked around the car for anything else of value. Besides the money and dope, Bear snatched the necklaces away from around Keysha's neck, and pulled the rings off her fingers. In a hurry, big Bear rushed from Keysha's car, and jumped into the front seat of Byron's ride. The second Bear slammed the door, Byron immediately sped out of the housing project. Bear couldn't wait another second to get his high on. He quickly went into the bag of coke ,and proceeded to snort a huge line. Ten minutes later, the two were pulling into Byron's driveway. The second he shut the car off, Byron looked Bear in his eyes, and asked the only question that was on his mind heavy at the time.

"Bruh, did you let that bitch live or nah?"

Bear simply glanced over at Byron, then went right back into the bag of coke for another line. He didn't utter a single word, which only made Byron ask the question again, only this time louder.

"Nigga! I know your big ass heard what the fuck I said!"

At that point, Bear let loose a loud, frustrated sounding sigh, then proceeded to respond to Byron's question.

"Woooo! Boy, if this dope wasn't so good, you would be blowing my high right now. But anyway, hell nawl, I ain't kill nodoby. I got the money and the dope, and got the fuck on, just like we had planned."

With a worried look plastered on his face, Byron slowly shook his head from side to side, as he began to reply to Bear.

"I understand what you're saying big boy but that broad peeped the lick and called it out. She ain't just gon let that shit ride like it's all good."

The second Byron finished his last sentence, Bear burst out with laughter, before he spoke his peace.

"Boy, stop. What she gon do? Go tell the cops somebody knocked her upside the head and stole her dope? Man, stop sweating that shit, and let's go inside, and enjoy this sack, while we count this fat bankroll of cash I got off ole girl."

Bear's words didn't calm his partners nerves whatsoever. At that moment, Byron still had heavy thoughts about Keysha's revenge l, and didn't have the urge to get high. However, he reluctantly went ahead, and snorted a line before exiting the car. Instantly, that clean, good dope hit Byron's soul, and made him even more paranoid than before.

While the two sat inside, counting cash, and indulging in the bag of cocaine that they had just stolen, Dunn Dunn was back in Bowling Park wondering what was taking Keysha so long to return to the trap. In between transactions, he quickly whipped out his cell to give Keysha a call. The phone rang and rang until it was answered by the voicemail. Immediately, Dunn Dunn pressed redial on his cell. Once again, Keysha didn't answer, and he was left listening to the voicemail. After the second attempt to reach Keysha failed, he began to worry even more. Dunn Dunn hollered from the front room of the trap into the kitchen, where Jit was standing over the stove.

"Ayyy, Jit! Jit!"

Without wasting any time yelling back and forth, Jit simply made his way to the front room.

"What up, Bruh?" Jit spoke in a curious tone after seeing the look in Dunn Dunn's eyes.

"I'm wondering where the fuck Keysha at. I gave her cell a couple of calls but got no answer."

At that moment, Jit's facial expression quickly matched the one Dunn Dunn was wearing.

"Yeah, that ain't like her not to answer. Let me try to hit her up, real quick."

Jit turned around and hurried to his cell that was back in the kitchen. After grabbing the phone from the countertop, Jit dialed Keysha's number. As he walked back into the front room, the answered sound of the ringing phone continued until the voicemail caught the call. Jit looked up and shook his head from side to side. His face frowned with confusion, and his forehead wore wrinkles from being puzzled about where Keysha was, and more importantly, why she wasn't answering. The two briefly sat in silence, as they both pondered what move to make next.

Suddenly, Jit's eyes lit up like the strip in Vegas. He had just remembered that Keysha's phone was on his contract, therefore he was able to track her location. Not even a full minute later, Jit looked at Dunn Dunn with confusion on his face, and spoke in an uncertain tone of voice.

"Ay, Bruh, it says right here that she's in Able Homes."

"Say no more." Dunn Dunn replied in a stern tone of voice.

In a haste, Jit and Dunn Dunn rushed from out of the trap, and were headed off to Able Homes Housing Projects. They sped the entire ride. Jit weaved his way thru traffic, as if he was a Nascar driver. Only ten minutes had passed by, and already they were only a block away from the projects. The second that Jit turned into Able Homes; Dunn Dunn spotted Keysha's car parked next to the trash dumpsters.

"Ay, Bruh, there go Keysha ride parked over there in the cut."

Jit pulled in directly behind where Keysha was parked. Just as the two were walking up to the car, Dunn Dunn saw blood on the seat, and Keysha's body slumped over inside. At that point, his adrenaline began to rush with panic. After seeing the blood, and her motionless body, his mind began to think the worse. Quickly, he snatched the front passenger door open, while Jit hurried to the driver's side.

The very moment that the fresh air hit Keysha's face, she slowly started to come thru. She placed her hand on the spot where Bear had slugged her across the head. The wet, sticky feeling of blood on her fingertips instantly made her nauseous and reminded her of how it all had happened. As Keysha attempted to make her way out of the car, her legs became weak, and she somewhat stumbled. Fortunately, Dunn Dunn was right there to catch her, and hold her up, until she fully gained her balance. In a concerned tone of voice, Dunn Dunn asked the only two questions that was on his mind.

"What the hell happened? Who did this to you?"

Both, Dunn Dunn and Jit stood eagerly waiting for Keysha's reply. Although, for the next few solid seconds, she was completely silent, as she replayed the robbery over inside of her mind. Keysha, then slowly shook her head from side to side, and in a drowsy tone of voice, she finally answered.

"Some nigga robbed me. I don't know who he was, but I think that fuck nigga, Byron set me up."

Soon as Keysha finished her words, Jit's face formed a furious frown, as he yelled out in an angry tone of voice.

"Byron! How the fuck he get close to you!?"

Keysha wore a shameful expression on her face, as she attempted to look up at Jit to respond. Knowing she was wrong for still serving Byron, she couldn't manage to make herself lock eyes with him. Keysha simply dropped her head, as she began to explain the situation.

"The nigga had hit me for an ounce, so I told him to meet me at the Fuel Tech at the corner of Forrest and Floyd Road. Soon as I got there, Byron hopped in the car, and everything seemed like it was all good. I went to weigh his work up, and the next thing I know, some nigga had snatched the backseat door opened, and planted a pistol to the back of my head before I had a chance to do anything."

Keysha paused her words, as Dunn Dunn interrupted her story with his own conclusion.

"Say no more. I may be wrong, but I do believe that punk, pussy ass, fuck boy was behind the lick. Whoever robbed you would not have gone thru with the move, after seeing someone else get in the car with you, unless he knew the person. That's just my opinion though."

There was a brief period of silence amongst the three, then Jit spoke.

"Keysha, I'm glad that you're okay, but you know that nigga Byron was cut off. He wasn't supposed to ever get served by us again."

Keysha knew what Jit was saying was nothing but the truth. However, before she had a chance to reply, Dunn Dunn looked at Jit, and spoke up in a commanding tone of voice.

"Ay, what's done is done. Jit you head back to the trap, get the money ready for the next package, and later, we'll figure out how to serve Byron's ass one last time, if you know what I mean. I'm going to drive Keysha to the hospital, to make sure she's straight."

After Dunn Dunn finished talking, Jit simply nodded his head in agreement, and began walking back to his car. Keysha sat back down on the passenger side of her ride, and Dunn Dunn got behind the wheel to head to the emergency room.

BACK AT THE COUNTY JAIL, with little to no emotions showing whatsoever, Ivory sat in the interrogation room with a stone face on display. He nonchalantly listened to all the bullshit the Feds had to say, but nothing seemed to rattle his cage. Of course, the attempt to lure him into snitching was quickly made, however that offer was declined just as fast. He softly chuckled when Agent Baxley mentioned the offer to set up Mr. Mexico, in return for his freedom. During Ivory's moment of laughter, Agent Conner bolted from the corner, and rushed across the room. With excessive force, he snatched the chair from underneath the table, then sat down next to his partner. Conner's face was fire hot red and flushing with frustration. While he looked deep into Ivory's eyes, he began to speak, and the tone of his voice boiled with anger.

"Do you know how much time you're facing!? Help us get something solid on your connect, or your ass is going to rot away behind bars!"

Ivory continued to chuckle, until Agent Baxley mentioned something that wasn't funny to him at all.

"Umm, Ivory, have you asked yourself how we knew where, and when to find you with a trunk full of coke?"

Ivory's eyes drifted upward, as he wondered where Baxley was going with this line of questioning. Just as he was about to give a reply, Agent Baxley fixed his face with a vengeful smirk, and proceeded to speak.

"No need to answer that question, Ivory. I have a better one for you. How well do you know, and trust Ms. Mea Morgan?"

Once the sound of the name Mea rolled off Baxley's tongue, Ivory's soul shivered. It was at that moment when reality truly started to set in. An image of Mea popped up in his head, and the thought of her snitching on him became embedded in his mind. He couldn't help but to replay the conversation that he had earlier with Ray. Silently, Ivory sat still praying that Mea's mouth wouldn't be the cause of his downfall. For the first time during the interrogation, the agents saw a glimmer of fear on Ivory's face. Agent Conner let loose an evil grin, as he looked at his partner then began to speak.

"Oh my, will you look at that, partner. Mr. Cool as an ice cube is over there melting by the minute now. Looks like he has a billion tiny beads of sweat running down his forehead."

With that same smirk on his face, Baxley spoke in a confident tone of voice.

"You're looking a tad bit shook there Mr. Phillips, as well you should. The ten to twenty years you're facing won't be easy for you to do. However, with Ms. Morgan's statement, and willingness to take the stand, it'll definitely be a piece of cake for the D.A. to prosecute you."

For the first time in his life, Ivory felt a flame of panic run through his entire body. He felt the sweat that Agent Conner spoke of trickling from his freshly shaved bald head. While wiping the perspiration away, Ivory cleared his throat, then finally responded in a firm tone of voice.

"You'll never break me. I don't care how much time you give me. I'll never snitch, not even on an enemy."

Agent Baxley looked at his partner with a blank stare on his face then shrugged his shoulders. Conner shook his head from side to side, then stood up, leaned in close to Ivory, and softly spoke.

"I respect being loyal but right now, you're just being downright stupid."

Before he even realized it, Ivory had rose from his seat, quicker than high school students when the final bell rings, at the end of the day. His brief panic attack had quickly turned into a hostile rage. One thing Ivory didn't tolerate from anyone was disrespect. At the moment, Ivory was just about to explode, when Jesup burst through the door, and spoke in a firm tone of voice.

"Don't say another word, Ivory!"

Immediately, Ivory's face that was just full of frowns turned upside down, and he calmly took his seat. Attorney Jesup quickly sat down beside his client, then whispered to Ivory. The words he spoke made a smile appear from ear to ear on Ivory's face. Finally, Jesup looked up at Agent Baxley and Conner, as if he had just won the lottery and spoke in a confident tone of voice.

"Well, being that this wasn't a routine traffic stop, my client wasn't presented the proper warrant to have his vehicle searched. He definitely didn't consent, therefore anything found inside is considered an illegal search and seizure."

Baxley and Conner looked at one another, and simultaneously began to laugh. True, they technically botched the initial stop, however they were banking on the fact that their informant, Mea Morgan would be ready to take the stand, if Ivory didn't plead guilty. Baxley continued to grin, as Agent Conner looked at Jesup, and began to speak.

"Okay, Jesup, normally you would have to wait for the discovery package to find this out, however I'm going to get straight to the point. Now, let me wipe that smug smirk off your face with the bit of information that you're not aware of. We have an informant that's ready to testify against your client. She's our key piece to putting Ivory away for a long time. Therefore, I suggest you talk things over, and decide how you wanna play it out."

Ivory didn't know what to think at the moment. He understood Attorney Jesup knew his shit, but he also knew Mea could lead to his demise. Just when Ivory seriously start sweating the situation, Jesup starred back at Agent Conner with a nervous look on his face and replied in a worried tone of voice.

"Umm, I see. Would you gentlemen please be nice enough to give me a few moments alone with my client?"

Agent Conner was now the one wearing the smile of a lottery winner. Before answering Attorney Jesup, he glanced over at his partner. Agent Baxley quickly shrugged his shoulders, indicating that he didn't have any issue with Jesup having some time alone with Ivory. Conner looked Ivory square in the eyes as he responded to Jesup's request.

"Sure, take all the time you need."

Just as Conner and Baxley stood up, the door to the interrogation room flew open. Their commander stood there with a disappointed expression on his face. He held the door open and waited for Agent Conner and Baxley to exit the interrogation room. The moment that the three men were all in the hall, Agent Baxley looked at their commander with a puzzled look on his face, then spoke with a heavy dose of curiosity in his tone of voice.

"Sir, why the long face? We'll get him to break soon."

The commander slowly shook his head from side to side and was about to respond. However, Agent Conner added his thoughts about the situation.

"I'm not sure if he'll roll over on Felix or not, but with Ms. Morgan's statement and testimony, we have enough to get him off the streets and behind bars."

The commanding officer stood with the same disappointed stare in his eyes, as he shook his head once again, and began to speak in a disgusted tone of voice.

"The witness is dead. Her body was just found in an alley behind the bus station. The trunk full of coke is inadmissible, because of the illegal search, therefore we're back to square one with Ivory."

"So, he's just gonna walk?" Agent Conner replied to the commander's news.

"Yes, once again, he's gonna walk. I'm leaving it up to you two to cut him loose." The commander confirmed Conner's question then gave instructions before slowly walking away himself.

"I just knew we had Ivory this time around!" Agent Baxley yelled out loudly, just before he turned, and punched a wall in the hallway. Agent Conner felt his partner's exact pain at the pit of his stomach. They both stormed up the hallway faster than a moving tornado and hurried back into the interrogation room. The moment that the two agents walked back in the room, the look on their faces displayed their anger and disappointment.

The second that Ivory made eye contact with Baxley, his cheekbones rose, and a smile brighter than the summer sun appeared on his face. He could tell that something had changed, from the time they last left him. Ivory continued to flash all thirty-two teeth, which quickly frustrated Agent Baxley even more than he already was. Another few seconds of silence went by, then Agent Conner couldn't take looking at Ivory's winning grin any longer. He briefly spoke his mind, before walking out of the interrogation room.

"You fucking disgust me, sitting there like you're really innocent."

The second that the door closed behind Conner, Ivory chuckled aloud, then ask a sarcastic and rhetorical question.

"Do you still see me sweating?"

Attorney Jesup quickly leaned over and whispered into Ivory's ear. He warned Ivory not to be overly confident and cocky. However, Ivory went on and continued to taunt Agent Baxley with another smart mouth remark.

"From the look on your face, Mea must not have anything to say now."

Once again, Ivory let loose a devilish grin and winked his left eye.

Agent Baxley reacted before he knew it. In a split second, he had exploded across the table and yanked Ivory up by the collar.

"Listen here, you low life, drug dealing son of a bitch! We don't have anything to hold you on today, however, I promise to bring your ass down one of these days."

At that point, Baxley shoved Ivory back down into his chair. Attorney Jesup looked up at the agent and spoke.

"If you're not charging my client or have nothing to hold him on, then this meeting is over."

Ivory and Jesup both rose from their seats and began to walk out of the interrogation room. Just as the two were near the door, Agent Baxley spoke one last time.

"Your day is coming, Mr. Phillips. And when it does, those cuffs aren't coming off. I promise you that."

Ivory paused at the door, turned back to face Agent Baxley and spoke his last words to the officer.

"You do your job, and I'm damn sho gon do mine."

Once again, Ivory walked out of the precinct a free man. Besides, seeing and holding Tweety, the most important thing on his mind at the time was seeing, and saluting his right-hand man Ray. Without Ray taking charge, and doing what had to be done, Ivory would be getting ready to do some serious time.

MEANWHILE, Bear was lounging up in Byron's apartment. He enjoyed watching his favorite movie, Scarface over and over, while he continued snorting the coke that he had stolen from Keysha. However, Byron wasn't at ease at all. It seemed like every line of coke that he snorted, his mind would drift back to thought of Keysha getting revenge against him. The look of fear was written all over his face, and honestly big Bear was getting irritated from seeing it. In a brut tone of voice, he firmly addressed the situation.

"Say, nigga, you still sweating that bitch and that lil lick we pulled earlier today?"

Byron quickly locked eyes with Bear and answered just as fast."

"You gotdamn right, I am. She ain't your regular as broad. This bitch got bodies under her belt. Plus, the crew she run with ain't no joke. Your ass been locked up for a while, so I know you dont know."

Bear squinted his evil eyes at Byron then laughed out loud just before he replied.

"Well, why the fuck you picked her to rob? But anyway, I know I've been gone for a decade but ain't nan bitch nor nigga in Bowling Park gon fuck with me, or you. Just chill."

Suddenly, there was a strong, thunderous knock at the door. Instantly, Byron's face painted a picture of panic, and his body froze up stiffer than a Macy's mannequin. He quickly glanced up at Bear, as the beating sound continued at his front door. Bear stared back at Byron with a nonchalant expression, as he spoke in a tone to match.

"Yo, Byron, are you gonna get that?"

Timidly, he tip-toed towards the front door, and looked through the peep hole. Byron saw two thuggish looking young men out in the hall-way. He turned and walked back to Bear then whispered.

"Ay, I don't know who the fuck this is at the door. Its two dark skinned, dread head niggas. Did you tell someone you would be here?"

Bear looked up in the air, trying to remember whether he did or didn't. A split second later, he then slapped the palm of his hand onto his forehead. As he began to reply, he rose from the couch and headed towards the front door.

"Damn, my bad, bruh. I told two young hustlers from my hood to come thru. They wanna check out the jewelry that we came up on today."

At that moment, Byron didn't say a single word. He was just relieved that it wasn't Keysha, and her crew knocking at the door. Bear opened the front door to the apartment, and the two guys began to stroll inside. Once they were in the living room, Bear looked at Byron and swiftly made the introductions.

"Ay, Byron, these my homeboys, Bird and Black."

Byron didn't verbally speak; he simply gave the two men a head nod then continued sitting on the couch watching television. Bird, Black, and Bear all made their way into the kitchen. Soon as the two-guest sat down at the table, Bear went into a high cabinet, and retrieved a small gym bag. He placed his hand inside and pulled out the pieces of jewelry that he had lifted from Keysha.

There were two lengthy, thick, gold, and shiny herringbone chains, a huge, and chunky rope chain, and a few gold rings dripping with diamonds. The moment the jewelry hit the table; Black dropped his mouth to the floor. Bear saw the look of lust in his eyes and knew this would be an easy sell. As they were admiring the chains and rings, Bear spoke up in attempt to sell more than the jewelry.

"Ay, do either of y'all need some good, clean coke? I got for the low low."

Black didn't react to the question at all, however, Bird quickly responded.

"Hell yeah! Let me see whatcha working with."

Bear didn't hesitate one bit. He went back into the small gym bag, and pulled out a digital scale, along with two ounces of the best coke in Georgia. Soon as the dope hit the table, Bird's eyes bulged up bigger than two bowling balls.

"Woo! Man, that's that pink Floyd cocaine, ain't it? How much for these two ounces?"

"Shiiid, if y'all get all this jewelry, I'll give you the two ounces of coke for the going price of one."

The next second, Black quickly spoke up.

"That's a done deal there. I wanna cop every piece of jewelry that's on the table, and I know my man Bird want that coke."

Bird grinned as he responded to Black.

"You already know, Bruh. Now, let's pay the man, and keep it moving.

Bird and Black combined their money and made the purchase. After the transaction was made, Bear began walking Bird and Black towards the front door. Just as the two were about to walk out of the apartment, Bird turned back around to face Bear and spoke.

"Say, you ain't got a pack of that loud, do ya?"

Bear quickly shook his head from side to side and replied.

"Nah, bruh, I don't have any. I mean, none to sell anyway."

Bear closed the door behind Bird and Black, then turned around with a giant Kool-Aid smile glowing on his face from ear to ear. The next moment, the big body dude began dancing, while counting cash all the way from the front door, back to the living room. Byron was still calmly sitting on the sofa watching television, but the thoughts inside of his mind were chaotic to say the least. Bear continued to hold his happy face intact, as he looked at Byron, and yelled out in a joyous tone of voice.

"Today was a good day!"

Big Bear flopped down on the sofa beside Byron, and once again, he started recounting the cash that he had just got from Bird and Black. After splitting the dollar amount in half, Bear extended his hand full of money towards Byron. The look in Byron's eyes expressed that he wasn't feeling nowhere near as happy as Bear. Slowly, Byron reached for his portion of the loot, and then just tossed it onto the table. Bear couldn't take Byron's miserable mood any longer without saying something.

"Ay, nigga, what the fuck is wrong with you? We got paid today, plus we still got coke to get high with. So why the long face?"

Byron swiftly turned his head towards Bear and locked eyes.

"Bruh, I just got a bad vibe telling me that our score from earlier is gonna come back on us."

"Nigga, I done told you not to sweat that shit."

Bear briefly paused his words, then an idea struck him out of the blue. He looked up in the air in deep thought, as he stroked the hair of his goatee. A second later, Bear began to share his idea with Byron.

"Listen, man. The best way to play this is to call ole girl now."

Byron's face formed a million frowns, as he interrupted in a sarcastic manner.

"Call her? And say what, nigga? I'm sorry, I had my partner rob you."

Bear smacked his lips, and quickly responded.

"Hell nawl. Listen, nigga. I'm saying, call her now, and act like you're concerned for her. Next, ask to cop a small sack of coke from her, since you got robbed the same time she did, and just see how she plays it."

Byron's face full of frowns quickly turned upside down as he replied.

"Well damn, that's kind of clever, big boy."

Byron didn't immediately make the call. He practiced the lines he would say, once she answered. After he was fully confident, Byron quickly whipped out his cell to give Keysha a call. On the third ring, Keysha looked down at the screen of her phone. She was totally shocked to see that Byron was calling. Keysha thought about answering, but then decided to ignore him, and send the call straight to voicemail. A second later, Keysha turned to Dunn Dunn and spoke.

"Man, you ain't gon believe who was just calling me."

At the time, Dunn Dunn was going in on a plate of oxtails, cabbages, and rice, as if it was his last meal. After spending a few hours in the E.R. with Keysha, he was starving. Dunn Dunn looked up from his plate, licked his fingers clean, then replied.

"Who dat?"

"Bitch ass Byron." Keysha quickly answered.

Dunn Dunn dropped his silverware in disbelief, then swiftly snapped back at Keysha.

"Why you didn't answer? Shiiid, if he call back, pick up, and see what the nigga got to say."

Soon as the last word rolled from Dunn Dunn's tongue, Keysha's cell started to ring again. Once she saw the caller ID flashing the same number, Keysha didn't waste another second, before she answered, and placed the call on speakerphone.

"Yeah, what up?"

"Hey, Keysha, I know you probably feel like I set you up, but that ain't the case. I'm just calling to make sure you were good, and also, I want to get a gram from you. That muthafucka got my money too, so that's all I got to spend at the moment."

The moment Byron finished talking, Keysha quickly locked eyes with Dunn Dunn. He had listened very closely to every word but didn't detect any bad vibe, that suggested he was lying. Dunn Dunn shrugged her shoulders and quietly spoke.

"Tell him to c'mon thru."

Without any hesitation, Keysha replied.

"Ay, Byron, I don't deliver small amounts like that, but you can come on to the trap, if you like."

"Bet. I'll be on the way in a few."

Byron ended the call with a completely different facial expression showing. He was thoroughly convinced that he was in the clear, after talking with Keysha. His smile now was almost as large as Bear's. Byron quickly locked eyes with his partner in crime and began to speak.

"Maaaaaan, you were right all along. I ain't got shit to worry bout now. After I shower up, I'm going across town to the trap. You wanna ride with me?"

"Bruh, unless they selling pussy over there, I'm gonna stay right here."

Bear cracked a smile, then continued to speak.

"Nah, I'm just fucking witcha. Uma ride Bruh."

Byron shook his head, and chuckled at Bear, as he made his way to the bathroom to freshen up, before heading to Keysha's.

WHILE ATTORNEY JESUP drove through the city, Ivory sat on the passenger's side, debating what his next move would be. He wasn't concerned at all about the last package getting seized by the police. Ivory had paid Mr. Mexico with diamonds, and there still were enough shiny stones remaining for him to leave the game and start a legit business with Tweety. However, Ivory couldn't help but think about Ray's and Jolly Jr's future.

For everything the two had done for him, Ivory owed them both dearly. He certainly wasn't the type to leave his people hanging. If one was ever loyal to Ivory, then he would always be there for them. A few more minutes passed by, and Ivory was so deep in a daze that Jesup had to loudly repeat calling his name just to get his attention.

"Ivory...Ivory!

Even after Ivory heard his attorney calling his name, he didn't verbally reply. Slowly, he simply turned his head towards Jesup and made eye contact.

"Yes, Ivory, I see you have a lot on your mind. Where would you like for me to drive you to?"

"Straight to Piedmont Projects, my projects."

As Jesup continued to drive, Ivory leaned back, and began to plot and play out his next moves in his mind. Now, Ivory was considering leaving the game, but not exiting without looking out for Ray and Jolly Jr. first.

Minutes later, the two were only a few blocks away from Piedmont Projects, when Jesup observed that an unmarked car had been following them for more than a few blocks now. As he somewhat nervously continued checking his rear-view mirror, Ivory finally noticed the unmarked car himself. In a calm tone of voice, he looked over at Jesup, and spoke.

"I see you peeping back at that unmarked cop car. Don't worry bout them at all, I'm too use to it now."

Jesup let loose a long sigh, then out of the blue made a u-turn in the middle of the street. Next, he once again looked up into his rear view mirror and saw that the unmarked car had got caught up in traffic. Jesup, then quickly maneuvered the car into a parking garage, and thru it into park. Ivory sat on the passenger's side of his attorneys ride with a grin on his face, and then jokingly made a remark.

"Damn, Jesup. You must been a race car driver, or something. But why the fuck you do all that? Ain't nothing illegal in here, is it?"

Ivory chuckled at his own words; however, Attorney Jesup wasn't in a laughing mood whatsoever. With a serious expression plastered all over his face, he turned towards Ivory and attempted to give him some great advice.

"Ivory, I know I'm just your attorney and not your father, but I do consider myself a true friend to you. With that being said, I seriously want you to consider getting out of your line of work. You've been more than lucky avoiding any lengthy stay behind bars, however in life, we all have periods when our luck runs out."

With all due respect, Ivory sat listening to each word Attorney Jesup had to say. After he finished speaking his peace, Ivory slowly nodded his head in an up and down motion, then replied.

"I understand what you're saying, and I'm actually thinking of getting out of the game. I just got to get some things lined up for the people that mean the most to me, and then I'm done."

Soon as Ivory ended his reply, Jesup didn't say another word. He simply put the car into gear and pulled out of the parking garage. A few minutes later, they were arriving at Piedmont. From the very first second upon entering the housing projects, Ivory's face formed a huge smile, a beaming glee glowed in his eyes, and his adrenaline automatically began to rush. The sight of a long line of customers that was formed in front of Miranda's apartment damn near made Ivory's dick hard. Without a doubt, he loved 'that life' fully and faithfully. From the nagging nickel buying fiends, all the way to the white-collar clientele, the love of the game always excited Ivory. Instantly, Attorney Jesup could see the change in Ivory's body language. What he viewed as a horrible, sad scene; Ivory saw a vision of beauty. When Jesup looked at the housing projects, he saw horrible living conditions, alcoholics, and drug addicts. On the other hand, when Ivory looked at Piedmont Projects, the picture was a portrait of home, and filled with people that admired him, and daily depended on help. He pointed towards a vacant parking spot, just below Miranda's place, indicating that's where he wanted his attorney to pull into. Once the car was parked, Jesup took a long, deep breath, and slowly exhaled. He then turned his head to the right and looked Ivory dead in his face. Jesup could see the star like glow dancing in Ivory's eyes. At that point, he didn't have the slightest bit of faith that his client wouldn't be a client again in the future. With concern written all over his face, Jesup spoke in a tone of voice that matched.

"Ivory, I truly do hope you consider retiring from your line of work. I'm great at what I do, and your loyal team saved you this time around, but a serious defeat is inevitable for this way of life."

Ivory understood everything Jesup was saying, but honestly, he didn't want to listen to anymore of his lawyer's lecture any further. In a harsh and cold manner, Ivory responded with the same lines that he had earlier recited to the Federal Agents.

"Listen, Jesup. You just do your job, and I'm damn sho gon do mine."

As he finished his words, Ivory was already opening the passenger car door, to hop out of Jesup's vehicle. Just before closing the door, Jesup said his final goodbyes.

"Take care of yourself, Ivory."

With the look of a cold-blooded killer, Ivory simply gave Jesup a head nod, then quickly slammed the car door shut. The next moment, he turned to make his way towards Miranda's house. After only taking a few steps, Ivory spotted Jolly Jr. coming out of the front door, and his face lit up with a smile brighter than high noon. Without any hesitation, Ivory yelled out in an excited tone of voice.

"JJ! What it do, Playboy!"

Once, Jolly Jr. saw that it was Ivory calling his name, he briefly paused in his tracks like a deer in headlights. Simultaneously, his mouth hung low and wide, as his eyeballs nearly soared from the sockets. It was as if Jolly Jr. had spotted a ghost. For a solid five seconds, his face wore a blank stare, while his feet stayed firmly planted in the same spot. Finally, Jolly Jr. snapped out of it and his face formed a smile that matched the one Ivory was wearing. As he proceeded to walk forward, he replied in a loud, joyous tone of voice.

"Ivory! Myyyyyyy Nigga! Whats good Boss!?"

Seconds later, the two greeted one another with a half hug, then Ivory replied to Jolly Jr.

"Shiid, I'm just thankful to be standing here with you, instead of being barred up inside of that county cage."

Jolly Jr. nodded his head up and down in a rapid pace, then replied to Ivory.

"Yeah, Ray was filling me in on a whole lotta shit that went down. I'm just glad to see you free!"

"Indeed. Is my man, Ray inside?"

"No doubt, he up in there."

Just before the two were about to enter Miranda's place, Ray was stepping out of the door. On sight of Ivory, his eyebrows rose damn near to his hairline. Although, his surprised reaction quickly turned into a joyous smile, as he embraced Ivory with a full hug. After the two parted, Ray held the same huge smile as he began to speak.

"Bruh, when Tweety hit my phone, and told me the news, it fucked me all the way up. I'm glad to see you Bruh, but with all them bricks you had in the car, I'm surprised they gave you a bond?"

The second Ray spoke the word 'bond', Ivory's face quickly froze up with frowns. He rapidly shook his head from side to side, then flashed his winning smile, as he corrected his right-hand man, Ray.

"Noooooo, no need for a bond, Bruh. All charges were dismissed."

"Well damn, that's really what's up there. That Jesup must have found a loophole to jump through?"

Ivory slowly nodded his head up and down, then began to reply to Ray.

"Oh fo sho! He did his job, and the law fucked theirs up. But you brought me to the house, when you sent that scary, snitch bitch Mea home. You feel me? Without you making that move, my ass would have been in a cage for at least ten years. Man, you were so right about that broad. I owe you, Bruh. I owe you everything."

Ray continued to lock eyes with Ivory, as he sincerely responded.

"Bruh, we're on the same page, and feeling the exact same way. If you wouldn't have put me on back in the day, I might be in a cage somewhere doing life myself, or already be dead by now. So please believe, I'll always be there for you, Ivory."

The two slapped hands and Ivory pulled Ray in for a half hug. Jolly Jr. was staring at the two with a look of admiration in his eyes. Ray and Ivory were like living legends in the streets, and now Jolly Jr. was ready to carve his name in the pavement. He loved the position he played in the game and was totally loving the team he played it with. Then suddenly, out of the blue, Jolly Jr. eagerly spoke up.

"Ay, say fellas, but what we gon do bout getting some work in? We down to the last of the last."

There was a moment of silence, then Ivory looked at Ray with a smile and spoke.

"That's a muthafuckin young soldier right there, and true to the game, bruh!"

Those words placed a smile on the face of Jolly Jr. that was wider than a billboard. Ray slightly grinned, then simply nodded his head up and down, indicating he totally agreed with Ivory. Seconds later, Ray dropped his smile, and asked the question again.

"But for real though, what up with the work?"

Without saying a word, Ivory started to walk into Miranda's. Just before he entered, he turned back around and spoke.

"Ay, let's go in the back room, roll up, and chop it up bout this work. I think I got something in mind that'll make life beautiful for everyone."

BACK AT THE trap in Bowling Park, Jit, Keysha, and Dunn Dunn were all making plays. The traffic coming in and out was non-stop. Easily, the three of them combined would have their re-up money in no time. As the day turned into night, briefly there was a moment where the clientele finally slowed down a bit. This was the first time that neither one of the three was making a transaction since they all returned. Dunn Dunn took this time to roll up his next few blunts. While he was breaking down the loud pack of weed, he glanced over at Keysha, and spoke.

"Ay, I can't hardly wait to look ya boy Byron in his face, when he come up in here. The eyes tell no lies, and his won't be any different. After one hard stare, I'll be able to tell if he was behind that lick or not."

Dunn Dunn had directed his words at Keysha, however, Jit was quick to respond in a bitter tone of voice.

"I can't believe the pussy ass nigga gon show his face in here, knowing he owe me for a whole zip."

Suddenly, there was a hard knock at the front door of the trap. Dunn Dunn quickly looked over at Keysha, then she turned, and stared at Jit. As the knocking continued, Jit was finally the one that rose to answer the door. After he looked thru the peep hole, he loudly smacked his lips, then turned back around to speak.

"Aww shit. It's just them two young ass niggas, Bird and Black. They probably just want a sack of loud."

"Well, let their young ass in. I'm trying to get back every dime that I got robbed for today." Keysha quickly replied.

Jit nodded his head and proceeded to let Bird and Black inside of the trap. The second that the two entered, Black didn't waste any time getting down to business. His eyes roamed around the room from Jit to Dunn Dunn as he spoke.

"Either one of y'all straight with that loud pack? We just trying to get a quarter sack."

"My homegul gotcha." Jit replied.

Keysha hurried up from the couch, from where she was seated, and dashed into the kitchen to grab her package of weed. Only seconds later, Keysha reappeared into the front room with the 7 grams of loud. As she walked up to Black, Keysha noticed the huge, chunky rope chain around his neck. Immediately, she felt a warm, rushing feeling run thru her soul.

The chain was a perfect match to one of the items that was stolen from her today. Keysha continued to gawk at the chain, as she handed over the sack to Black. The moment he extended his hand out to give Keysha the cash, her eyes got bigger than the breast on a young Dolly Parton. She recognized the gold ring, flooded with diamonds, that Black was wearing on his pinky. The second their hands touched for the exchange, Keysha held on tight, and began to speak in an angry tone of voice.

"Look, man! I don't know what the hell going on, or who the fuck you got the chain, and ring from, but that's my shit you got on!"

Soon as Keysha finished her words, Dunn Dunn stood with the swiftness, and proceeded to pull out a handgun from his waistline. Bird and Black now were in the trap feeling trapped. Black's mouth was wide opened, however not the first sound was coming out. Jit then pulled his pistol out, and began to inch even closer to the door, just to block Bird and Black off from trying to leave. There was a brief period of silence, then the distinct sound of Dunn Dunn cocking his gun sent nervous chills up the spine of Black. Once, Dunn Dunn loaded his weapon with one in the chamber, Black's fear caused him to seriously stutter, as he attempted to calm the situation.

"Wait, wait, wait, now... no, no, no need for the guns." Black panicked as he spoke.

Keysha snatched him closer to her, then wildly yelled at him, to the point saliva flew all in his face.

"Where the fuck you got my shit from!?"

At first, Keysha's question went unanswered for a few solid

seconds. Dunn Dunn then walked up on Black, and put the gun to his temple, which quickly got a response.

"Don't shoot Bruh, please don't shoot. I, I, ... I bought these pieces off an OG from around my way earlier today."

Just as soon as Black stopped talking, Dunn Dunn pressed the gun against the side of his head even harder, then demanded more details.

"Look, young nigga, I don't give a fuck bout this gun going off and painting the walls with your gotdamn brains. The best thing for you to do is to tell me who the hell your OG is, and where the fuck he laying his head at right now."

Black rapidly nodded his head up and down, indicating that he fully understood what Dunn Dunn was saying.

"I don't know his real name, but he go by Bear."

Keysha cocked her hand way back and let loose a slap across the face of Black that stung so hard, to the point, it even left a handprint on his dark skin complexion. The next second, she then loudly screamed at him.

"Didn't you hear my nigga ask, where the fuck he laying his head at!?"

As Black began to answer, he held his hands up in the air, pleading for this situation not to further escalate.

"Ok, Ok, Ok. I really don't know the dude that Bear is hanging with, but his name is Byron. I just met him today. They're over at his place now."

Simultaneously, Jit and Dunn Dunn looked at one another, and shook their heads side to side. Keysha pulled the ring off Black's hand, and took the chain from around his neck, then asked one last question.

"Where the rest of my shit at? My chains, rings, and the dope!"

Black cut his eyes over at Bird, then hung his head down as he mumbled an answer to Keysha's question.

"The other chains and rings are out in the car, but we don't know anything about no dope."

Jit opened the door then proceeded to walk Black out to the car to retrieve the rest of Keysha's jewelry. Dunn Dunn moved over towards Bird, and looked him up and down, as if he was about to seriously do some bodily harm. However, after a few seconds of strictly intimidating Bird, he calmly posed a question.

"How much ya boy paid for the jewels?"

"Two grand." Bird quickly replied.

Dunn Dunn let loose a devilish grin, then quickly wiped any trace of a smile off of his face, as he stared into Bird's eyes and spoke.

"Now, when yo boy come back in here, if your answer don't match his, then it's gone be a serious price of pain to pay."

At that exact moment, Bird knew he had fucked up. All he could do now is say a silent prayer for Black to be on the same page as himself. Seconds later, Jit was marching Black back into the trap. The moment they both were inside; Dunn Dunn didn't waste any time. He began walking up on Black with a look that pierced his soul, and placed fear into his heart. Black stood there with the remaining jewelry in hand, shivering in a frantic panic, as Dunn Dunn approached. They were only inches apart from one another when Dunn Dunn leaned in and began to speak.

"Aight, look, and listen, this is what's about to happen. I'ma whisper a question to you, and then you're gonna whisper the answer back to me."

Black nervously nodded his head up and down, then Dunn Dunn leaned in closer and softly spoke.

"How much did you spend in all?"

"A grand." Black whispered back.

The moment Dunn Dunn heard the answer, he spun around on a dime, and aimed his gun directly at Bird's head. At that point, Bird's heart sank to the pit of his stomach. Keysha yelled out at Dunn Dunn, encouraging him to escalate the situation.

"Dead that muthafucka! Gon blast his ass, Bruh!"

Just before Dunn Dunn started to reply, Bird began to beg for his life, as he saw it flash before his very own eyes. With a devilish smirk on his face, Dunn Dunn continued to enjoy watching Bird plead for mercy on his soul.

"Please, don't shoot! Please, I'm begging you, Bruh! Pease don't kill me!"

Dunn Dunn tightened the grip of his gun, and began to take steps towards Bird, as he replied to his pleading cries.

"Nawl, young nigga, I ain't gon kill you bout some gold ya boy bought, but I am gon shoot your ass for lying to me."

With that being said, Dunn Dunn dropped his aim away from Bird's head, and lowered it towards his legs. The next second, a single shot was fired, striking Bird in his right kneecap. At the point of impact, the bullet began to brutally burn, as Bird quickly fell to the floor in agonizing pain. Black was still fearful for his wellbeing, as he stood holding the rest of Keysha's jewelry in hand. However, he immediately dropped the chains and rings, as his reactions pushed him across the room to help his friend stand back up. As Bird clung onto Black, Dunn Dunn stepped up closer, and began to speak to them both.

"You would've got your money back, if your man here would've just been real and told the truth. And yo dumb ass could've walked out of here, but you were too stupid. Now hobble your simple, silly, lying ass up outta here."

Unbeknownst, to anyone on the inside of the trap, Byron and Bear had just pulled up into the parking lot outside. After, Dunn Dunn spoke his mind, Black and the injured Bird began to make their way out of the trap. However, before they were able to make it to the exit, there was a knock at the front door. Jit was standing the closest, therefore he yelled out.

"Who dat!?"

"It's me, Byron!"

Before anyone could say a word, Jit had opened the front door and pulled Byron inside. Jit spun him around, then yanked him up by the collar. It happened so fast that he didn't even notice anyone else was there besides Jit. With his back facing the room, immediately, Byron began to apologise for not paying back the money for the ounce Jit had fronted him some weeks back.

"Listen, Jit, I'm sorry, man. I didn't intend to stiff you. Bruh, shit just got crazy."

The same moment that he finished speaking, Keysha yelled out from across the room.

"Hell yeah, fuck boy, shit bout to get real crazy!"

As Jit let him loose, Byron quickly turned his body around towards Keysha's voice. At that moment, Byron saw Bird and Black making their way out, then he really knew that he had truly fucked up. Byron couldn't get a word out, not that anything he said would be a benefit to him at that point. Jit closed the door behind Bird and Black, then shoved his gun into the middle of Byron's lower back, and forcefully proceeded to walk him across the room. Seconds later, Byron was standing face to face to Keysha. There wasn't a single sound in the room, until Dunn Dunn jokingly broke the silence.

"Since, I already done shot one nigga today, I'ma just kick my feet up, and watch this shit."

Keysha starred at Byron with fury in her eyes, as she debated on how she would start to torture him. First, she pulled her gun out, and placed it flush against the center of his chest. She cocked the weapon back, but suddenly lowered the tool down to her side. Keysha had an idea pop up in mind, as she flashed an evil grin, then quickly dashed towards the kitchen. Seconds later, she reappeared holding a huge hatchet, with a 12inch blade. Byron's eyes bulged out from the socket, like a jack in the box. He desperately pleaded with her to let him live.

"Keysha, I'm sorry. Let me leave here breathing, and I promise I'll pay you back double for everything."

Before Byron knew what happened, he found himself on his knees with a throbbing pain at the back of his head. Jit had struck him across the dome with the butt of his 9mm. As he looked down at Byron, he yelled at him with vengeance in his tone of voice.

"Nigga, you didn't pay me back for a straight up deal! So, you know ain't no way you gon get a pass to straighten this bullshit out that you tried to pull!"

Keysha stepped forward, calmly placed the tip of the blade underneath Byron's chin and lifted his head in the air. She looked him square in the face and began to shout out instructions.

"Ay, get your lame ass up, and go sit on the couch beside Dunn Dunn!"

With his hand still holding the lump Jit had just put on his head, Byron slowly made his way over to the couch. Once he was seated, Keysha continued to shout in his direction.

"Now, put the palms of your hands on the gotdamn table!"

Once again, Byron's level of fear shot up quicker than summertime temperatures in Georgia. His hands were nervously trembling as he extended them out onto the coffee table in front of him. As Keysha began making her way over to the couch with the hatchet in hand, Byron begged for her not to do any harm to him.

"Please, Keysha! Don't cut off my fingers!"

"No nigga! I ain't gon cut off your fingers, I'm chopping at your muthafuckin wrist."

In the same split second that she finished her reply, Keysha raised the sharp, wide, kitchen blade above her head, and aggressively came down with all her might. As the knife pierced Byron's skin, it split into the bone. However, the blade became wedged in the middle, before it could cut the wrist off clean. Keysha quickly yanked on the handle and pulled the blade out.

Byron screamed out in pain, then instantly became nauseous at the sight of his dangling wrist, and gushing blood. Once again, Keysha, raised the hatchet high, and was about to come down to finish her deed, when suddenly the door to the trap damn near came flying off the hinges. The big body of Bear barreled through the doorway, bussing bullets with precision. Best believe, by the time anyone could react, Bear had the whole gang in grave danger. Before Dunn Dunn could rise from the couch to reach for his gun, Bear had already let loose a hot one that grazed Jit's shoulder. Just as Dunn Dunn was about to grab his weapon, Bear had already drawn down on him. As he let one loose, he yelled in Dunn Dunn's direction.

"Touch that gun, and the next shot going in your skull!"

Dunn Dunn had no real choice, but to ease back, and place his hands in the air. However, when Bear turned his gun on Keysha and ordered her to throw down the knife, Dunn Dunn took his chances, and dove for his gun. Bear spun around and let off a shot that missed Dunn Dunn's head by less than an inch. Bear went to fire another round off, but his weapon jammed, and wouldn't fire. Keysha had slid over and had her hatchet ready to chop, as Dunn Dunn now had his gun aimed, and ready to fire. At that moment, Bear couldn't do anything but surrender. He shook his head from side to side, as he dropped his weapon to the floor. A second later, Dunn Dunn demanded the two to leave, while they still had a chance.

"Y'all muthafuckas get to stepping before I get to blasting!"

In a haste, Byron and his dangling wrist headed towards the door, as Bear and his 300-pound frame followed right behind him. Suddenly, just before the two could make their exit out of the trap, the sound of four-gun shots echoed throughout the room. Jit had squeezed off at the two, as they were making their way out. Three shots dropped Bear's big body right there in the doorway, and one bullet hit Byron dead in his ass.

Keysha burst out into laughter at the sight of seeing, Byron squirming and screaming as he hobbled in a hurry, out of the trap door. Dunn Dunn slightly shook his head from side to side, as he joined in on the laugh with Keysha. Meanwhile, Jit was still standing with his gun in hand, and a mean mug on his face. He was far from being in any mood to laugh. He stared at Dunn Dunn, and Keysha with the look of sheer seriousness stuck on his face, as he raised his voice in a disgusted tone.

"What the fuck y'all find so funny!? I don't see shit to be laughing about!"

Dunn Dunn continued to chuckle, then with a friendly smile on his face, he replied to Jit.

"Calm down, cowboy. Everything all good now, bruh."

Those words didn't calm Jit down at all. If anything, Dunn Dunn's nonchalant response only made Jit angrier about the whole entire situation. His face frowned with fury, then he shook his head from side to side in a highly irritated manner. Jit then locked eyes with Dunn Dunn and replied.

"How the fuck you figure everything all good? You done shot one nigga in the kneecap and made an unnecessary enemy. I had to lay this big body muthafucka down here, after you were bout to let him leave. And on top of all that, I'm standing here with my got damn shoulder burning from a bullet going through it."

Jit briefly paused his words as he glanced over and stared at Keysha. He then raised the volume of his voice, as he began to chastise her in an upset tone.

"First of all, you are serving junky, crab ass niggas like Byron! That's what caused all this to pop off any got damn way!"

In a frustrated manner, Keysha, momentarily dropped her head into the palms of her hands, then suddenly, she sprung from her seat. In a flash, she ran up into Jit's face, and replied in a tone of voice that matched his.

"Nigga, I said my bad for that earlier! Yeah, I fucked up, but damn! It is what it is now!"

Before Jit could reply, Dunn Dunn stepped in between the two, and demanded them to calm down.

"Ayyyy! Both of y'all, cool the fuck out!"

For the next few moments, a strong hush of silence fell over the room. Dunn Dunn and Keysha both took a seat on the sofa, while Jit couldn't keep still. With his pistol still in hand, he continued pacing from one side of the room to the next. Then, suddenly, Bear's body showed signs of movement. He slowly tried to stand up. After, he finally made it to his feet, Jit aimed his gun directly at Bear's head. A split second later, an idea crossed Dunn Dunn's mind and he quickly spoke up.

"Hold up, Jit! Don't shoot!"

Jit didn't squeeze the trigger, but he also didn't drop his aim. He continued to hold a tight grip of the gun, as he quickly cut his eyes over at Dunn Dunn and replied.

"What the fuck you mean!?"

"Shiiiid, we might can use big boy." Dunn Dunn quickly responded.

A few seconds passed by, as Jit allowed Dunn Dunn's words to sink in fully, then he lowered his gun and placed it back inside of his waisteline.

Dunn Dunn looked in Bear's direction and yelled out.

"Ay! Big boy you wanna job, or do you wanna die?"

Bear was big, and strong as an ox, but at the moment, he swayed from side to side, heavy bleeding and barely breathing. His body had absolutely no balance whatsoever, as he used the wall to hold his gigantic frame up. He was obviously near blacking out, but Bear was conscious enough to realize his life had just been spared. As Dunn Dunn proceeded to speak, he gave out instructions as he glanced back and forth from Keysha to Jit.

"Aight, let me put a plan together, and see what y'all think about it. Keysha, I want you to stay here with me, and we'll handle getting the rest and of the pack gon, and the re-up money ready. Jit, I'll help you load big boy up into your ride, and y'all go to the hospital to get some attention to those bullet wounds."

Jit didn't verbally say a word; however, he quickly nodded his head up and down, indicating that he was in agreement with Dunn Dunn's plan. Keysha knew Bear wasn't aware of who she was when he came to rob her earlier, but she still felt some type of way knowing that he would in some form, or fashion be on the same team as her. However, she didn't voice her opinion. She glanced over at Jit, as he agreed to the plan, then jokingly spoke.

"That's what it is then. Now, gon to the hospital, and get a bandage put on that lil scratch of yours."

Jit still wasn't in a laughing mood, however, he had nothing but love for Keysha, therefore, he managed to make a small smile appear on his face. Of course, Dunn Dunn giggled at Keysha's remark, as he made his way over to assist Jit with loading Bear up. After the two finished struggling with the 300+ pound body, Jit was ready to take his place behind the steering wheel. Just before Dunn Dunn turned to walk back into the trap, Jit looked at him, and spoke in a calm but serious tone of voice.

"Listen, bruh. I didn't mean to be seeming salty, or nothing like that. It's just I always want us to stay on top of our game, so we gotta stay on point at all times. The bigger we get, the bullshit gon get bigger."

Dunn Dunn nodded his head up and down in agreement, then replied before walking back inside.

"We good, bruh. And regardless of how big the bullshit gets, we gon always be bigger."

AFTER, Ivory sparked up a blunt, larger than the average black man's dick, he passed it to Ray, then began to speak in a serious tone of voice.

"Aight, I'ma get straight to the point. I been playing my role in this game for years. Now, the only part left for me...is to leave it behind before it takes me under."

Quietly, Jolly Jr. sat there with a wide-eyed look of admiration on his face, clinging to every word that Ivory had to say. However, Ray's facial expression only consisted of a confused frown that had formed, after hearing Ivory's decision. He didn't really like the direction this talk was headed whatsoever. Just as Ivory was about to continue speaking, Ray spoke up instead.

"Yo, what you trying to say, Ivory?"

"I'm bout to fall back from the streets, bruh." Ivory, quickly replied.

With a super shocked expression showing, Jolly Jr. looked at Ivory, as if he had just spoke in a foreign language. Ray slowly hung his head into the palms of his hands. He honestly didn't know how to respond to the words that Ivory had just spoken. Then suddenly, within the next split second, Ray held his head high again, and attempted to give a good enough reason for Ivory not to leave the game behind.

"You can't leave now though. The cops just got the whole damn re-up package of work. You gotta make that right, cause I know you ain't trying to run off on the plug."

After Ray finished his words, Ivory didn't hesitate replying at all.

"Bruh, that package was paid in full from the second I picked it up. I had been debating with myself for the last trip, to really be my last trip, so I put my own money up."

The second after Ivory was done replying, a silent hush hit the room. Ray didn't want to even think of living 'that life', without Ivory being the heart and soul of it. During the moment of silence, his mind started to race at a rapid pace. Ray sat back in his chair and took a long, hard pull from the fat blunt, then slowly exhaled before passing it on. Ivory could clearly read the look of disappointment that was plastered on Ray's face, and he also noticed the lost, shocked expression that Jolly Jr. had on his. At that point, Ivory truly began to feel the depressed vibe that was flowing in the room. He slightly put a small smile upon his face, then attempted to lift the spirits of his comrades.

"Fellas, y'all looking like I said I had cancer, or something. My run in the game's up, not my time on Earth. Besides, I ain't gon just leave, without leaving both of y'all super straight."

The last sentence Ivory spoke caused Ray and Jolly Jr. to simultaneously look up at one another. In a blink of an eye, their facial expressions had completely transformed. Instantly, Ivory felt the drastic mood swing in the room, which made him crack a smile himself. Ray eagerly sat on the edge of his seat, as he awaited to hear the rest of the plan. Just before, Ivory continued to speak, Jolly Jr. spoke up in an excited tone of voice, as he rubbed his hands together.

"Shiiid! What you got for a young nigga, Boss?!"

Soon as, Jolly Jr. asked his question, Ray briefly dropped the smile from his face. He wasn't at all pleased to hear the sound of greed. He quickly cut his eyes over at his young partner in crime and shook his head from side to side in a slightly disappointed manner. However, Jolly Jr.'s extremely overanxious choice of words only made the big boss grin. After a brief laugh, Ivory turned towards Ray and began to speak.

"Look, bruh. Since I came up in the game, you've always been there for me. I could never repay you for your loyalty nor your actions however, I can and will introduce you to the plug."

Ivory's words put a look in Ray's eyes that resembled the winner of the mega million-dollar lottery. Before he even realized it, Ray had jumped to his feet, flowing with excitement. He had played his part as Ivory's right-hand man through thick and thin, and now, he was being rewarded the greatest gift a dope boy could ever wish for. Jolly Jr. also happily rose out of his seat and onto his feet. He slapped hands with Ray, then sincerely began to speak, as he looked his partner square in the eyes.

"Congrats, bruh. I know I'm young, and all but I'ma be here for you, just like you were always there for Ivory. Believe that."

Ivory quietly looked on at the two, as he stroked the hairs of his goatee. After hearing the words that Jolly Jr. spoke to Ray, Ivory's face lit up with a smile brighter than the summer's sunshine. He slowly nodded his head up and down, as he held his joyous facial expression. Ivory was now feeling that he was making the best move by leaving the game behind. Just as Ivory stood from his seat, there was a loud, knock at the front door. Ray quickly glanced over at Jolly Jr. and spoke.

"Ay, check and see who that is knocking. We just selling breakdown pieces right now though, until we get another package in. We ain't sitting on enough weight to do much else."

Jolly Jr. hurried from the back room and dashed down the hallway. As he made his way through the front room, he yelled out in a loud voice.

"Yeah, who that!?"

"Nigga, open up the damn door and see!"

Jolly Jr. burst out into laughter, at the sound of the familiar voice. As he reached his hand down towards the doorknob, he responded to the person standing on the other side of the door.

"Fast Freddie!"

Once Jolly Jr. opened the door, Freddie was standing there dressed in his dirty oil-stained mechanic suit, with the stench of alcohol flowing heavily from his breath. He wore a crooked smile on his aging face, as he held some crumpled up cash in the palm of his hand. As he stepped inside of the trap, Freddie spoke in a joking manner.

"Where my bitch, Miranda at?"

"Shiiiid, somewhere in one of these projects over here, probably doing the same thang you're about to get into. But anyway, what you trying to grab?"

"The usual, two for thirty, Playboy. Two for thirty, if you can stand it." Freddie responded in a humble tone of voice.

Soon as Freddie replied to Jolly Jr., Ray entered the room and answered in a stern tone of voice.

"Nah, Freddie, not today. Your lil two for thirty deal is on hold, until we get the next package in."

In a flash, Freddie's face lost any trace of a smile. He was beyond bothered by the words he just heard, and truly wanted to start talking shit about not getting his usual deal, however, Freddie knew better. He wouldn't dare attempt to speak to Ray, in the same tone of voice as he use to do Frost. Therefore, he simply nodded his head up and down, then extended his hand out that held his money. Jolly Jr. took the thirty dollars from Freddie, then darted towards Miranda's room to get the dope. A few seconds later, Ivory entered the front room with the burning blunt hanging from his mouth. The moment Freddie saw Ivory, his smile magically reappeared, and his body began to do his favorite dance. As Ray and Ivory both laughed at the "junky, bout to get high" moves that Freddie was performing, Jolly Jr. was walking back into the room with the dope in the palm of his hand. As Freddie continued to dance his way towards Ivory, he spoke up in a confident tone of voice.

"Now, I know you gon give a dog a bone. Hook me up, Ivory. Two for thirty, my man."

Ivory quickly cut his eyes over at Ray, then looked into Freddie's face and spoke.

"Nah, Freddie, I can't do it. You just got the word from the man who's running everythang. I'm out the game now."

Freddie's face formed a blank stare, as he couldn't believe what he had just heard. On que, Jolly Jr. walked up to Freddie, and put the piece of crack rock into the palm of his hand. After, he got his dope, he was still standing with his mouth hung wide open, in total disbelief of what he just heard. Freddie shook his head in disgust, as he turned to make his way towards the door. Just before he walked out of the trap, he spun around on a dime and spoke in Ivory's direction.

"Yo! What the fuck you gon do besides sell dope, though?"

Freddie didn't wait for an answer before he dashed on out of the door, however his rhetorical question was left looming heavy in the room. There was a lengthy period of silence where everyone just seemed to be off in a daze of their own. Suddenly, Jolly Jr. looked at Ivory with curiosity written all over his face, and then he spoke in a manner that matched.

"Say, Ivory, like for real for real, what you got planned, Boss? I mean, what you gon do after giving up the game?"

In anticipation of hearing the answer, Ray nearly snapped his neck, as he turned to look over at Ivory. The question that was asked, instantly brought heavy thoughts of Tweety to mind, which certainly put a smile on Ivory's face. He couldn't hardly wait to get home to her but first he wanted to finish his business in the streets. Another few solid seconds passed by, while Ivory simply stared towards the ceiling, and steadily stroking his goatee. He could clearly see legally living each day with Tweety, with no worries of losing his freedom or life to the game. It was time to retire, and finally Ivory had started to look forward to his future. Just as he was about to completely drift off into a total daze, Jolly Jr. spoke again, which snapped Ivory back from his daydream.

"Ay, Boss, I'm just saying, I can't believe you're just gon give up this life. I mean, you got all the money, power, and respect and just gon walk away from it?"

As soon as Jolly Jr.'s words reached Ivory's ears, his forehead flooded with wrinkles from the force he frowned his face. The way that Ivory felt, if he was never a part of the game again, he would always have plenty money, power, and forever be respected. He slightly shook his head from side to side, as he stared across the room. The very next moment, just before Ivory was about to begin his reply, the sound of gunshots filled the room. Simultaneously, everyone on the inside of the trap dropped to the floor quicker than a stripper on the pole. Like hard, tropical rainfall pouring down, plenty pieces of shattered glass from the blasted front room windows flew inside of the apartment. A split second later, another large number of rounds were let off. Immediately following that barrage of bullets bursting from barrels, Ray jumped up from the floor with his gun in hand. However, by the time he made his way outside, a large, black cloud of burning rubber is all that he could see, and the loud, screeching, squeal of tires peeling out of Piedmont Projects is the only thing he could hear. In a haste, Ray spun back around on a dime, and dashed back towards the trap. Just before he reached the door, Ivory and Jolly Jr. were both coming outside. In a concerned, and jumpy tone of voice, Ray was the first to speak.

"Everybody good? Ain't nobody hit?"

"Nah, we straight." Ivory quickly replied.

The sound of gunfire had brought everybody out of their apartments. For a minute, the middle of Piedmont was looking like they were having a fire drill for the whole entire projects. Seconds later, Freddie and Miranda were headed through the crowd of onlookers, on their way back over to the trap. The two were walking at an extremely fast pace and fussing amongst themselves. After Freddie spotted Ivory,

Ray, and Jolly Jr. on the porch, he yelled out in their direction, as he walked up with a look of dismay expressed on his face.

"Man! Them muthafuckas came for y'all asses then! They had to let off a hundred rounds, or more!"

"And ain't hit shit!" Ray quickly replied in a firm tone of voice.

"They came, but they didn't come correct." Jolly Jr. added his two cents, then Ivory spoke up and asked the key question at hand.

"Yeah, but who the fuck is they? That's what we need to be focused on finding out."

Before anyone could respond to Ivory's words, Freddie pointed his finger in Miranda's direction, as he quickly spoke up.

"She says, she know who it was. Yeah, Miranda swear it was some of ole girl folks that stay across from her."

All at once, everyone turned and looked at Miranda. With a stunned look on her face, she stared straight into Ivory's eyes, and began to speak in a nervous tone of voice.

"Now, Ivory, I ain't trying to get caught up in some shit where I could catch a bullet."

Before, Miranda could continue her words, Ray abruptly interrupted her. With the swiftness, he had pulled and pointed his gun directly at the temple of her skull before she could even react. In a frozen stance, Miranda stood stiff as a mannequin, while Ray loudly responded in a tone of voice filled with aggression.

"You could catch a bullet right now, while you bullshitting!"

Immediately, Ivory stepped up and signaled for Ray to lower his weapon. With a cold hearted, gangsta's stare spread across his face, reluctantly, Ray slowly put his gun back onto his waistline. Once, Miranda saw the gun disappear, she then took her first breathe since it was pulled and pointed at her head. As the soul of eyes bubbled with fear, her body language expressed the exact same sentiment. Ray was still staring at Miranda with evil intentions in mind.

He didn't want to waste any time with games, he only wanted answers. He truly wanted to start torturing the shit out of Miranda until she spilled her guts, however, Ivory addressed the situation with a totally different approach. He stepped up even closer to Miranda, then gently placed his right index finger underneath her chin. Slowly, Ivory lifted her head upwards until her eyes locked with his. He calmy placed his left hand upon her head, and slowly stroked his fingers through her hair, as he started to speak in a softer tone of voice.

"Listen, Miranda. The sooner you tell me who pulled this shit, the less you have to worry about."

Ivory then placed the palms of his hands against the trembling cheeks of Miranda's face, and stared deep into her eyes, as he continued to speak in the same soft tone of voice.

"Now, tell me what you know."

Soon as Ivory finished speaking, he let loose of the soft grip that he had on her face. Instantly, Miranda began nodding her head in and down, indicating that she was ready to talk. Just before opening her mouth to speak, she attempted to compose herself by taking a deep, long breath. After slowly exhaling, Miranda finally began to speak.

"It was Quan and Duck, Mea's first cousins from Mayfield Projects."

The second that Miranda gave up the names and a location, Ray gave a head nod to Ivory, then bolted towards his car. Ivory stood there with a slightly frustrated frown on his face, as he shook his head from side to side. He had wanted to make the call to Mr. Mexico, to get Ray and Jolly Jr. situated for future business. However, now that would all just have to wait. With a cold, silent stare on his face, Ivory dismissed Miranda with a simple hand gesture. He then turned towards Jolly Jr. and spoke in a commanding tone of voice.

"Look, bruh, c'mon and drive me to Tweety's."

Without another word exchanged, the two were off and on their way.

WHILE IVORY WAS HEADED home to his Queen, she was already there, sitting on the sofa, worrying herself half to death about him. With each moment that passed by, the sips of wine she took, eventually turned into gulps. Unfortunately, the buzz that the booze brought, only darkened her thoughts with doubt. Since, being cut loose by the cops, Tweety hadn't heard a word back from Ray, nor Jesup. Therefore, she had seriously started to think the worse. However, unbeknownst to her, Ivory was free as a bird in flight, and only a matter of minutes from walking through the front door.

Tweety had started on her second bottle of wine, when she decided to roll up, and spark another fat one to help calm her nerves. To her, the last six hours felt like it had been six days. She took hard, long tokes from the blunt, and held every bit of the smoke, before slowly exhaling. As Tweety sat during a cloud of loud, her mind drifted off into a daze of pain. She started to feel the hurt in her heart, from losing her loved ones to the game. Her father, Hernandez, who she loved so dearly, was gone too soon because of the game. Her best friend, Mea, lost her life for breaking rules of the game. And now, Ivory was just taken away from her, as he was trying to leave the game. Safe to say, Tweety now truly believed in the saying, "ain't no love in the game."

It had grown late into the evening, but Tweety decided to give Jesup and Ray another call. Whether the word was good, bad, or ugly, she desperately needed to know, if there was any updated news on Ivory's situation. The first phone call she attempted was to his attorney. A split second after Tweety pressed send on her cell, the call was sent straight to Jesup's voicemail. While the recorded sound of the lawyer's voice played, Tweety let loose a loud sigh of frustration. As she waited for the beep to leave a message, the ringing of her doorbell caught her completely off guard.

Without leaving a message, Tweety ended her call, as she sprung from the comforts of her couch, and hurried towards the door. With each step that she took across her glossy, hardwood finished floors, the more her mind wondered, who was the unexpected guest out on her front porch. Once, Tweety made it to the door, she quickly looked through the peephole. On sight of the person standing on the other side of the door, Tweety's heart dropped to the pit of her stomach, as her soul shivered. In a startled manner, she jumped back away from the peephole, as if she had just seen a ghost. Her mind was wildly racing with thoughts, and for a few solid seconds, Tweety simply stood there in a complete state of shock.

In attempt to somewhat compose herself, she took one long, deep breath, and slowly exhaled. Just as Tweety wrapped her soft hand around the brass doorknob, the ringing of the doorbell sounded once again. At that point, she no longer hesitated. Tweety decided to open the door, but verbally didn't greet her guest with any welcoming words whatsoever. For a brief moment of time, the two stood face to face without either making a sound. Finally, the person standing outside of the doorway boldly broke the ice.

"Well, are you going to invite me in or what?"

The very moment those words hit Tweety's ears, she nearly lost total control of herself. Now, with the meanest of mugs expressed on her face, Tweety stared at the person on her front porch with a look of evil in her eyes. In a loud and angry tone of voice, she furiously snapped back with a response.

"Invite you in!? Why the fuck would you even think that I would want to see you?"

Tweety briefly put a pause to her rant, as she watched the unwelcome guest sadly hang their head in a disappointed manner. Honestly, Tweety somewhat enjoyed seeing the painful expression that was painted on her unwelcome guest's face. It was the exact same look of hurt that Tweety had to live with for the most part of her life. The second that the guest held their head back up, Tweety continued her rant in the same loud and angry tone of voice.

"You left us fifteen years ago! Fifteen years! What kind of woman walks out on her husband and leaves her 12-year-old daughter behind!?"

Soon as Tweety finished speaking her mind, her mother's mouth dropped down to the doormat. She couldn't believe what she had just heard. She had a different story and pleaded with her daughter to give her the opportunity to tell it.

"Is that what you think happened? Is that what your cold hearted, bitch ass daddy told you? I promise you, baby girl, that's not how it went down. Please, Tweety Bird, just let me in and give me a chance to explain it all."

Tweety was now feeling a bit more than confused. The genuine manner in which her mother spoke seemed so real to her. The sincere look in her eyes had no trace of a lie at all. The whole vibe was telling Tweety that she may have been misled about the details surrounding her mother's exit out of her life. However, since she was twelve years old, Tweety only knew her father, Hernandez as being a parent.

He was the one that was always there for her, supporting her emotionally, and financially. Hernandez faithfully showed his daughter unconditional love, and for that reason alone, he would always mean the world to her. Tweety always felt that her mother, Jasmine gave up the right to be called a parent, the moment she left her behind. Tweety still hadn't moved a muscle to let her mother through the door, although she was curious to hear her mother's version of the story. With a look of pure pain pouring from her eyes, Jasmine, once again asked to enter.

"Tweety, please let me in to talk. I would have never just up and left you. Please, I'm begging you."

Seconds later, Tweety calmly took a step back and allowed her mother to walk through the door. Jasmine entered the 5,000 square foot home, and her eyes bulged with amazement. The high ceilings were perfectly designed, and the enormous crystal chandeliers sparkled beautifully. As she followed her daughter over towards the front living room area, she complimented the exquisite oil painting of Tweety and Ivory, which elegantly hung above the wood burning fireplace.

"Oh my, that's one gorgeous painting you have there."

Jasmine briefly paused her words and continued to marvel over the artwork on the wall. Suddenly, her eyes squinted up, as she looked at the details of the painting. With a shocked expression plastered on her face, Jasmine proceeded to speak in a tone of voice to match.

"Wow! Is that man in the painting the same boy you use to be so crazy about in Jr. High?"

The question only made Tweety think of Ivory, and their situation even more. Without confirming whether, or not the man in the painting was indeed Ivory, Tweety took a seat on the sectional, then lifted her glass of wine from her glass coffee table. She took another large swallow, then finally looked over at her mother, as she replied in a slightly irritated tone of voice.

"Look, lady, I didn't let you in my house for us to kick it, like we're cool, or sum. Just say what the fuck it is you gotta say!"

Tweety kept the same frustrated frown on her face, as she stared at her mother. Jasmine simply nodded her head up, and down in a rapid motion, then softly began to speak.

"Tweety Bird, I love you with all of my heart. And again, just know, I would have never just left you behind if I had a choice."

Tweety abruptly interrupted Jasmine. She didn't wanna hear all that love talk, she just wanted to know why her mother left her behind and where she'd been for the last fifteen years. At the top of her voice, Tweety yelled out the only questions she wanted answers to.

"Fuck all that shit you talking bout! Just tell me why the hell you left us, and where the fuck you've been!"

At that moment, Jasmine rose from the couch, and exploded in the same manner, in which Tweety had just spoken.

"First of all, whether you acknowledge it or not, I'm your gotdamn mama, so show some fucking respect, lil girl!"

Jasmine briefly paused her words, as she stared into her daughter's eyes. She calmly took a seat back down on the sofa, then proceeded to talk to Tweety.

"Baby girl, I didn't walk out on you. I walked into something I didn't see coming. True, your father came along and got me out of the streets from prostituting myself, however, he also introduced me to the dope game at the same time. Fifteen years ago, I was arrested for trafficking ten kilos of coke for your father. Come to find out, the buyer of the bricks was an undercover agent. Once I was booked and processed, I called your father to come put up the bond money. He said he would be down asap and have me out within an hour. But yeah, that hour turned into fifteen long years of hard prison time. I know I wasn't the most faithful wife, but I didn't think he would just leave me for dead like that."

Jasmine paused her words to wipe away the tears from her eyes. The emotional story that she was telling not only made her cry, but it also had Tweety starting to whimper. She felt terrible for hating her mother for all those years, and she felt betrayed by her father. Jasmine extended both of her hands out towards Tweety and instantly, she grabbed a hold of them. With a pure vibe of love flowing, she pulled her mother close for a warm, embracing hug. For a moment, the two sat in total silence holding one another. The next minute, Jasmine let loose a long sigh of relief, then stared Tweety in the eyes and continued to speak.

"Now, I'm not expecting you to change up on your father. I fully understand you loving him because he was the one always here for you. But I am asking to be a part of your life again. Those fifteen years in chain gang taught me a lot. Thankfully, my heart learned to forgive, even if I can't forget. With that being said, I don't have any ill will towards your father. How is he by the way?"

At that point, Tweety truly believed every word that had rolled off her mother's tongue. As she painted a picture of her father in her mind, Tweety slowly shook her head from side to side. The sad thoughts of the day she got the news of her father's demise had resurfaced. Before answering Jasmine's question about Hernandez, Tweety hung her head low, then seconds later, looked back up, and into her mother's eyes, then finally replied.

"Ma, you really didn't have any communication with the outside world for all of those years. I feel horrible for not having a chance to be there for you. I'm really feeling some type of way about Daddy right now, but I'm sorry to say, he was killed in a drug deal gone wrong, up in some part of Tennessee."

"Umph, umph, umph. He cost me fifteen years of my life cause of the game, then end up losing his life to the game. I would say that's karma but baby, it just ain't no love in that game."

Jasmine's last choice of words sent a cold chill throughout Tweety's soul. The mood of her spirit was like a rollercoaster ride, at the moment. She was hurting from thinking about Ivory sitting in a cell, like a caged animal. She felt joy from her mother's return, and at the same time, she felt a piercing pain at the pit of her stomach from thinking about how her father had lied to her for all those years.

Jasmine was thrilled to be home, and even more excited to be sitting with Tweety, but she couldn't help but to see the agony on her daughter's face. It was highly evident that her heart was dealing with a tormenting situation. In a caring tone of voice, Jasmine broke the brief period of silence.

"Baby, you seem like something is heavy on your mind. Is everything alright with you?"

Instinctively, Tweety gazed up at the painting of her and Ivory, that hung over the fireplace. Automatically, the question that Jasmine had just asked, sadly made Tweety think of having to live her life without him. From that thought alone, it nearly brought her to tears. Just before she began to reply to her mother, Tweety reached over into the ashtray and re-lit the blunt. As she held the flame from the lighter to the end of the cigar, she spoke in a saddened tone of voice.

"The same game that took you away from me, just took my man as well. I haven't heard from him since we were arrested."

"We?" Jasmine quickly replied in a surprised tone of voice.

"Yes, Ma. I said we, as in us. I've always been Ivory's ride or die."

Upon hearing Tweety's response, Jasmine's eyebrows rose to the top of her forehead. A split second later, she replied.

"I hear that, child. Well, at least he didn't have you out here driving dope around by yourself."

"He didn't have me doing anything. He really didn't even want me around the shit at all. I'm just so hurt because we had plans for today to be the last day in the game."

Jasmine vividly saw the love Tweety had for Ivory. It was heavily pouring out from the look in her eyes, and she felt the pain from the hurtful tone of her voice. She placed one hand inside the palm of her daughter's, and her other hand on top, as Tweety continued to vent.

"I wanted to start my own hair salon. I was gonna have a nail shop in there, plus a couple of stations for on duty make-up artist. And my man was behind me one hundred percent. Daddy had left his club to Ivory, but he was ready to transform that to make my dreams come true."

Jasmine slightly tightened the grip of Tweety's hand and responded in a steern tone of voice.

"Don't you dare sit here and talk that way! I don't wanna hear such phrases, like I wanted to, I was gonna... child, please. You still can do it. I understand the hurt of missing a loved one. I truly do, but he'll be even more proud of you, if we get that shop started up. Hell, put me in station. I been locking hair for the past fifteen years."

Jasmine slightly chuckled at her own words. Just as Tweety was about to start her reply, once again, the ringing of the doorbell sounded. Tweety seriously frowned up in the face, as she shook her head from side to side. She had no idea who could be at her door, but she wasn't in the mood to see, or talk to anyone else. Tweety bolted up from the sofa and stormed towards the door.

Without asking who was there, she forcefully snatched the door wide opened, and was good and ready to start cussing somebody completely the fuck out. However, when she got an eye full of who was standing there, her mind was cleared on sight. Her face began to gorgeously glow, and instantly, her heart was healed of all pain. Ivory was home, as well as her mother, who she thought she would never see again. Just when Tweety was feeling that she had lived the worse day in the history of any human being on Earth, it certainly didn't end that way. Her pretty smile now stretched as wide as the doorway that she was standing in. As she happily gazed into Ivory's eyes, she could vividly see the joy he was feeling as well.

He stepped closer to Tweety, and tightly embraced his arms around his lovely lady's waist. With ease, he scooped her up from the ground, then she wrapped, and locked her legs around the small of his back. Ivory proceeded to carry Tweety a few steps back inside of the house. After, he placed her back down, and her feet touched the ground, the two locked lips for a long, passionate kiss. Ivory ran his caressing hands down Tweety's back, and tightly squeezed her beautifully shaped behind.

He gripped her ass with the strength of a python, as he moved his lips away from hers, and started to gently nibbling, and kissing upon her earlobe. Tweety softly moaned out sounds of pure pleasure, as Ivory maneuvered his lips, and tongue up and down her neck. Suddenly, out of the corner of his eye, Ivory noticed a middle-aged woman that bared a striking resemblance to Tweety's Mama. She was sitting on the sofa and grinning, as she stared at the cute couple. Slightly startled, and a bit embarrassed, Ivory cracked a blushing smile, as he let loose of the tight embracing hug that he had on Tweety. The second that he released his lady from his arms, Tweety finally remembered her mother was in the room herself. After opening the door, and seeing Ivory there, she was so overwhelmed with emotion that she had completely forgot. Tweety giggled like a happy little schoolgirl does about their first love. She gazed back up into Ivory's eyes and quickly spoke, before turning towards her mother.

"Ivory, you remember my mom, right?"

Honestly, the only real memories Ivory had of Jasmine was listening to Tweety talk about her after she left her, and Hernandez behind. However, on his face, he held his charming smile in place, as he began to walk over to greet her. Jasmine rose from the sofa with open arms, and embraced Ivory with a hug, as she spoke in a friendly manner.

"Hello there. How's everything?"

"I can't, won't complain. I'm just thankful to be here." Ivory replied, as the two separated.

Jasmine nodded her head up and down, then replied in an agreeing manner.

"I hear that child. I'm feeling absolutely the same way."

From across the room, Tweety looked on at the two with pure delight dancing around in her eyes. The smile that she wore on her face was just as bright as the future she planned to have with her family. Without question, Tweety was much more than pleased to have her mother, and her man under the same roof.

Happier than a kid on Christmas morning, she strolled over towards Ivory and Jasmine. As she approached her man, she gently placed her hand inside of his, and interlocked their fingers. Tweety then performed a bit of a fake yawn, then proceeded to speak in her mother's direction.

"Well, Ma, you can pick any bedroom downstairs that you like. I think me, and bae bout to lay it down for the night."

The second Tweety finished her line, Jasmine briefly broke out into laughter, then replied in a sarcastic manner.

"I bet y'all two bout to really lay it down. Shiid, I need to be somewhere laying it down myself. It's been fifteen years, child."

Instantly, Ivory laughed out loud, while Tweety stood with a blushing smile on her face. As Ivory continued to find humor in Jasmine's remarks, she once again spoke.

"Your laugh reminds me every bit of your father's. Is he still living around these parts anywhere?"

After Ivory heard the words she spoke, all sounds of laughter ceased, and any trace of a smile quickly vanished from his face. He attempted to maintain his cool, calm, and collected demeanor, however thoughts of his father sent flames of fury flushing thru his soul. As if, he was standing out in the summertime sun in Georgia, small beads of sweat began to pop, and pour from his forehead. Tweety, immediately noticed the change in Ivory's vibe, and she also knew why.

Back in the day, when Ivory was thirteen, his mother left for New York, in pursuit of her singing career, however after quickly becoming addicted to heroin, her dream chasing, as well as her life tragically ended. Ivory had blamed his father for letting his mother go alone, and never forgave him. Up until he was fifteen years old, Ivory and his father lived day to day, check to check. They were just as broke as any other family on his block.

Around the same time, Tweety had started pinching from the pounds of weed that her father, Hernandez had laying around, to give to Ivory to flip. Ivory's father hated dope of any sort, and even more, he hated dope dealers. The bigger Ivory grew in the game, the less the two had to say to one another. It had been over ten years since they last spoke. Occasionally, they would see one another in the neighborhood, but neither would bother to acknowledge the other. Jasmine stood awaiting a reply from Ivory, however it was Tweety that spoke up instead.

"Yes, Mr. Phillips still stays in the same apartment complex. I ran into him the other day down at the fruit market."

Jasmine also had noticed the look on Ivory's face, after she had mentioned his father. Once, Tweety ended her white lie, her mother quickly replied.

"Oh okay, maybe I'll see him around town soon. Well, I won't hold you two love birds up any longer. We'll talk more in the morning."

"Good night, Ma."

Tweety felt a joyous feeling from being able to say that to her mom, and only after taking a few steps, she felt Ivory's strong grip that he placed on her right cheek. As he squeezed even tighter, he used his other hand to give Tweety a slap on her left cheek. She gently bit down on her bottom lip, and in the sexiest of manners, she strutted her hour-glass shaped figure up the stairs.

The moment the two entered the room, Tweety dropped her robe to the floor, and proceeded to walk over to the bed. Ivory salivated at the sight of her thick, apple bottomed shape behind, as it bounced across the room. Tweety laid on her back, and in a seductive manner, she opened her legs. While, her eyes were locked onto Ivory's, she licked her lips, then softly spoke.

"Come get this pussy."

And for the next hour, Ivory did just that. From soft, slow strokes, to a deep dick pounding, he thoroughly pleased her pussy, until the two climaxed together. Tweety's face wrinkled with pleasure, as she collapsed onto Ivory's chest. He wrapped his strong arms around her beautiful body, and they both fell asleep for the night.

THE NEXT MORNING, Tweety was the first in bed to awake. The very second that she opened eyes, she quickly glanced up at Ivory. Instantly, she smiled from ear to ear, as she simply stared at his closed eyelids. For a moment, Tweety watched her man peacefully sleep, before quietly getting out of bed. Once her feet hit the floor, she yawned, stretched, and began wiping the cold from her eyes. As she proceeded to walk across the room, she replayed the pussy pounding Ivory had put on her the prior night.

Tweety thru on her silk robe, and slid into her designer house shoes, then headed towards the bathroom. After she brushed her teeth, and washed her face, she decided to get in the kitchen, and chef up a big breakfast meal for Ivory. As she made it halfway down the stairs, the alluring aroma of bacon being cooked hit her square in the face. For a split second, Tweety stopped dead in her tracks, and inhaled a nose full of the delightful smell. Once she made it downstairs, and to the doorway of the kitchen, she saw her mother standing over the stove, dressed in the same outfit from the prior night. Jasmine was whipping up some eggs, stirring the grits, and flipping the bacon, all while singing, Sam Cooke's classic, "A Change Is Gonna Come".

Just for a brief period of time, Tweety quietly stood in the doorway, and admired the sweet tone of her mother's angelic voice. The sound coming from Jasmine's mouth was undoubtedly beautiful to her, and the agony in her mother's heart could clearly be heard, as she sang the lyrics of the song. Once again, Tweety started to think about the years her mother had spent away from her. All her life, she had been under the impression that she was the one getting the short end of the stick, by her mother not being in her life.

However, she couldn't even attempt to imagine how hard it was to do fifteen years of prison time, without any love and support. Suddenly, Jasmine spun around to grab the butter from the refrigerator and was totally startled by Tweety's presence. With a shocked expression on her face, Jasmine gasped out loud then began to speak.

"Wooo! Damn, girl you bout scared the shit out of me!"

Tweety slightly giggled, then went on to apologize, as she began to respond.

"Oh, I'm sorry Ma..."

Momentarily, Tweety paused her words, and suddenly, her face was now wearing only signs of seriousness. She walked closer towards her mother, as she proceeded to speak."

"...and Ma, I'm truly sorry for not being there for you, while you were locked up. I just didn't know."

Immediately, Jasmine put the butter down. In a haste, she stepped closer to her daughter, and placed her hands on Tweety's shoulders. Jasmine stared her in the eyes and spoke in a stern tone of voice.

"Listen, Tweety Bird. What's done is done. The past is just that, the past. I'm just thankful for my fresh start at a new life, and excited about the times we can now share together."

Tweety smiled in a joyful manner, and quickly nodded her head up and down. She then replied to her mother in an excited manner, and tone of voice to match.

"And those times are going to start today. Uma see what all Ivory has planned, but me and you are going on a girl's day out. Mani and pedi, a full body massage, followed by a strong shopping spree. We must get you back right."

Tweety stood with an expression that defined happiness, while Jasmine's face lit up brighter than the nights sky on the fourth of July. She was happy that the reunion with Tweety was off to a great start. While smiling from ear to ear, Jasmine opened the cabinet, and retrieved three plates. As soon as she began to set the table, Ivory walked into the kitchen, already fully dressed, and ending a phone call. After putting away his cellphone, with a friendly smile in place, he glanced over, and greeted Jasmine, as she continued to prepare the spread of food.

"Good morning."

"Good morning, Ivory." Jasmine replied in a pleasant tone of voice.

Ivory then began making his way over towards Tweety. As he stepped in her direction, she stared into his eyes with a look of pure seduction. Tweety instantly became moist at the sight of Ivory. Before the first word was exchanged between the two, he tightly wrapped his arms around her waist, and gave her a passionate kiss. Suddenly, Jasmine spoke up from across the room.

"Ok, if you two can keep your hands off one another long enough to eat, then c'mon take a seat at the table. Breakfast is ready."

As soon as Tweety began to take her first step towards the table, Ivory discreetly tugged on her robe from behind. He quickly leaned over her shoulder, then started to softly speak, just a tad bit louder than a whisper.

"Ay, baby, uma have to skip out on breakfast this morning. I got Ray waiting on me. I wanna get some of this street shit in line, and out the way, so I can truly call it quits."

Tweety spun around with a smile on her face, and joy oozing from her eyes. The sound of hearing Ivory talk about leaving the game gave her ears an orgasm. She reached her arms up in the air for a hug, and the two quickly embraced one another. Soon as their bodies separated, Tweety began to reply with her plans for the day.

"Ok, Bae, that sounds beautiful. I think uma take Ma out to do some shopping, after we eat. We'll probably be out, and about all day, but just give me a call, if you need me for anything."

With an odd expression heavily glued onto his face, Ivory slowly nodded his head up and down, as he stroked the hairs of his goatee. He looked over at Jasmine, and polietly said his goodbyes.

"See ya later on this evening, Mrs. Barkley. You and Tweety enjoy the day together."

Next, Ivory quickly tilted his head towards the living room, indicating that he wanted Tweety to walk him to the door. The second that the two were out of the kitchen, Ivory started to question Jasmine's intentions.

"Say, Tweety, you sure bout all of this?"

"Of course, Ivory. I'm too ready for you to leave the game behind." Tweety quickly answered.

With a slight frown on his face, Ivory rapidly shook his head from side to side, then responded.

"Nah, I'm not talking bout me. I'm talking about your moms."

Suddenly, the gorgeous, glowing, bright smile that Tweety was wearing, instantly turned dimmer than darkness. Her eyes bulged and batted after hearing what was on her man's mind. Easily, Ivory could read her thoughts, simply from the look on Tweety's face. Before she had a chance to ask, why was he questioning his mother's intentions, Ivory continued to speak.

"Look, I'm just saying. I'm not in the business of trusting too many people anymore. Everybody just be out for themselves. Besides, how she just pops up out of the blue? And where has she been all these years?"

Tweety slightly rolled her eyes, and smacked her lips, then replied.

"Ok, I get it, Ivory. Your first cousin, Frost betrayed you, and Mea turned out not to be trustworthy, but baby, please believe me when I say Mama is being one hundred."

Ivory's eyebrows rose, as he slowly nodded his head up and down, before responding.

"Aight, Love. I hear you, even though you ain't answer nan question that I asked you. Uma get on up out of here and try to go get some shit handled. You be safe."

As he leaned in for a goodbye hug, Tweety embraced Ivory, and started to speak.

"Ok, Bae, I will, and you do the same. We'll talk later about Ma, and you'll understand after I tell you the whole deal."

Ivory gave his lady a quick kiss on the lips and then was on his way out of the door. Tweety briefly stood there biting down on her bottom lip and reminiscing about the way Ivory had made her cum so hard, so many times last night. Seconds later, she snapped out of her daze, and headed back towards the kitchen to have breakfast with her mother. The moment that Tweety took her first step into the kitchen, Jasmine spoke.

"So, he's thinking that I'm here to use you, and to leach off of y'all? I hope for your hearts sake that he's really gone quit selling dope, but I don't know child."

Tweety simply smiled, as she continued walking towards the table to take her seat. She was happy and wasn't going to allow anything to steal her joy. She wasn't letting Ivory put any negative or cautious thoughts into her head, and she wasn't about to let her mother's doubts about her man leaving the game to enter her mind. Tweety only flexed her smile a bit harder. As her beautiful cheekbones rose, she calmy began to reply to Jasmine.

"Oh, Ma, it's nothing personal, at all. It's just that Ivory has true trust issues. He's really been done wrong by a few people that were supposed to be close to him, so now he's a bit more cautious. But anyhow, enough of all that. Let's just enjoy this beautiful breakfast you've made and then get ready for a lovely day of shopping."

Made in the USA
Coppell, TX
02 April 2024